I0599050

UNBEARABLE MAGIC

MAGICAL MIDWAY PARANORMAL COZY SERIES, BOOK #3

LEANNE LEEDS

BADCHEN PUBLISHING

Unbearable Magic
Published by Badchen Publishing
14125 W State Highway 29
Suite B-203 119
Liberty Hill, TX 78642 USA

UNBEARABLE MAGIC

CONTENTS

CHAPTER 1

"The Werebear Jamboree, ma'am," Aldo Forest responded as he sat down across from me. It was Friday, and I was receiving complaints, petitions, and conversing with anybody that requested to speak with me. I had introduced our new, formalized open-door policy at the Magical Midway. I hoped it would encourage our citizens to see themselves as active participants in the circus's future.

Aldo had come with a request.

"Every ten years, all bear shifters gather on the top of Big Bear Mesa to celebrate our culture. Everyone at the Magical Midway is invited to attend, of course. Our festival is known worldwide for our Salmon Cook-off competition," he said proudly.

"Oh! Sorry, I'd never heard of it."

"Of course not. You're *not* a werebear, and you settled in the human world," Aldo informed me and cleared his throat. "It's why I informed you about what it was."

At some point, I would be here long enough to not have my sordid human past recounted in *every* conversation by paranormals that still seemed slightly miffed I didn't pop out of the womb in a circus costume.

"I appreciate you educating me, Aldo." I smiled. "Are you letting me know all the bears will go, or…?"

"Actually, ma'am, Brenda, Billy, Honey and I had a family meeting, and we wondered if you would consider relocating the Magical Midway to the Werebear Jamboree *during* the festival," Aldo said as he leaned forward. "There are a lot of children at the festival, and I'm sure many of them don't even know what a circus is, considering so many grow up in paranormal towns these days."

"Are you sure? Don't all the townie paranormals think we're all a little strange with our teleporting nomadic selves and human visitors? I'd presume that would include werebears."

"Perhaps some do. It seems to me that you aspire to change that, ma'am," Aldo pointed out and held up his hands.

I nodded.

"I think this would be a tremendous opportunity to do it with one part of the public. Every werebear in the world aspires to attend, and most do."

He has a point, Charlotte, Samson said. He rolled over on the shelf and stretched his head upside down off the side. *You and Gunther can snuggle in a room and plan for the world to change all you like. At some point, you must go out to shake hands and kiss babies. May as well start with paws and cubs. They're cute. From a distance.*

We don't snuggle.

You might be in a better mood if you did.

"Let me talk to Uncle Phil about the schedule, and make sure we're not blowing off any important commitments. If we're not, I think it's a great idea."

"Splendid!" Aldo pushed himself up and held out his hands. "Now, I wish to hug you, as you have made me feel festive and delighted." He beamed at me with his big, bulky arms stretched wide.

I had also encouraged each paranormal group to share their uniqueness with others, to feel more comfortable bringing their natures out into the open (as long as it could hurt no one else).

Apparently, bears like to hug. Who would have thought?

"The Werebear Jamboree is reputed to be *quite* the celebration," Uncle Phil said, once I located him in Jeannie's Snack Shack.

"I would *love* to go, Phil! I would discover so many new things to make for the shack! Their Salmon Cook-off is supposed to be *transcendent*," Jeannie told Uncle Phil as she cleaned up her counter. "The start of the festival is a salmon-catching contest, and all the salmon caught fresh is used in the cook-off."

"That's a *bunch* of bears jumping in a river." I snatched a pink pickle off my uncle's plate.

"Only the biggest and strongest bears compete, so not as crazy as you would think. They also have a children's event for the cubs." Uncle Phil took his plate from the counter and swatted my hand. "You leave my pickles alone. Jeannie can grant you your own."

"I'm good. I just wanted that one."

"It might be a good break for us. At least at the Jamboree, we won't need to worry about the Witches' Council," Jeannie said. Uncle Phil nodded. "They tend to avoid those big paranormal gatherings."

"Why?"

"Too much concentrated *other* power in one place. Remember, it's just the three of them that poof all over making trouble for everyone with magic. Mostly, they control the paranormal world by the laws, and by targeting anyone that becomes a threat to their power."

"You mean by fiat, not laws," I grumbled.

"Isn't that a sports car?" Jeannie asked as she leaned against the counter. "A Fiat? I think I granted one of those once..."

"It's an arbitrary order. The word, I mean. Fiat the car's name came from an acronym for the car company."

"Superb, Charlotte!" Uncle Phil said, beaming. "I'm very impressed that you knew that."

"Girls like cars, too, Uncle Phil."

"One day you should have Jeannie grant you a vehicle. You and Gunther could go on a drive through the countryside. Get away from here for a bit. I think it would do you both some good."

"Yeah, it might be nice to get out of the yurt for a change."

"You two have been working very hard," Jeannie said. "Have you come up with a plan for the next Witches' Council meeting?"

"We're still working on it."

Working on it wasn't really the word for it.

When Gunther and I became lawgivers, it seemed like the most brilliant idea in the world. We would become part of the legislative process. We would right the wrongs of the paranormal world. We would serve as a check on Mina's arrogant leadership, helping the paranormal world take its first steps toward more freedom. We would create a kinder and gentler society for supernaturals everywhere.

Then Gunther and I studied paranormal political history, and our idealism popped like a balloon punctured by the pin of reality.

"He's a very handsome young man, Charlotte," Jeannie teased, pulling me back from my daydreams. "It's a wonder you can concentrate on anything at all when you're sitting next to him. I've granted wishes that weren't as cute as that young man."

"We're just working on the lawgiver thing, Jeannie. He's a friend. I have enough on my plate right now without the complications of a relationship." I averted my eyes and stared out of the window hoping the subject would change. Quickly.

"Of course," Jeannie nodded. Her eyes moved over to Uncle Phil, and she softened. "All great love stories should start out like that. I know mine did."

Uncle Phil stepped forward to fold Jeannie into his arms, and he kissed her on the top of her head. They gazed at one another fondly and then turned back, still arm in arm.

"No love here," I told them. "Just friendship."

"Of course, Charlotte," Jeannie smiled. "Just remember, dear, you're living as a witch now. Destiny has a way of finding paranormals just when we expect it's not looking for us."

"I've had enough destiny for one lifetime, Jeannie. Destiny needs to go bother someone else for a while."

"Oh, destiny can expand beyond lifetimes, Charlotte," Uncle Phil smiled at me. "I'm proof of that. In any event, the Werebear Jamboree. I think it's a marvelous idea. Let's do it."

~

Salmon.

Be silent.

Salmon.

Samson, I swear, you must be quiet. Let me focus.

Salmon salmon salmon.

"Oh my gosh, will you just shut up!" I yelled out loud at the cat and heaved a pen at him. Samson scrambled like mad to evade the projectile and knocked down a stack of books, and a lamp, with a deafening clatter.

Not my fault.

Shut up.

"Um…is there something I can help you with?" Gunther asked, glancing up from a crumbling parchment. His face bore that bemused expression that caused my heart to skip one or two beats. With one eyebrow lifted and a half smirk on his face, Gunther would have made any woman swoon.

Ahem. Except for me. I don't swoon.

"Sorry. Samson can't wait for us to move to Big Bear Mesa tomorrow. All I can hear is the word salmon echoing in my head. Over and over. Loudly. I can't concentrate on anything we're looking at. I'm just frustrated, that's all."

"My parents took me to that when I was younger," Gunther said, leaning back in his chair. "If you've never been, it's enjoyable. They have drum circles and tree climbing contests. And Samson is right, the salmon is extraordinary. A lot of the bears own five-moon fish restaurants in paranormal towns, and they have some amazing chefs."

"Five moons?"

"It's the highest number of moons you can earn."

"At least salmon is healthy. Sounds like we'll be eating a lot over the next week. I could use a break from funnel cakes and cotton candy."

"My mom loved the Jamboree," Gunther said as he gazed off into the distance. After a few seconds, he turned back. "Anyway, you should make sure someone lets the ghosts know they can come out and meander around while you're there."

"Oh?"

"The Jamboree is on a mesa. They'll be shielded from view. No one can get up there if they're human, and the tree cover is pretty dense, so no one has to worry about planes or helicopters or anything."

"I still don't get why they never come out of

the haunted house," I told him, closing the book I was reading and stretching my aching shoulders. "I went to talk to them about a solution to their being locked up all the time, they insisted they were happy where they were."

"Ghosts can be a little strange. They really can go anywhere and do anything, but most of them stick to a location or a house or a place, sometimes for years. No idea why, but it always seems to happen that way. I think time feels different to them." Gunther nodded toward my stretching arms. "You sore?"

"Yeah, being stooped over these books day after day is not doing my posture any good."

"I'd be happy to rub your shoulders if you'd like. I give a pretty good massage. At least that's what some folks have told me."

Nothing was inappropriate in Gunther's offer, statement, or voice, but what he said made butterflies in my gut all the same. I leaned forward and put my chin on my hands. "Do you do that on purpose?"

"Do I do what on purpose?" he asked.

I'm taking off, Samson said as he jumped down and headed toward the door. *There is no way I want to be here for this exchange.* Delilah meowed and hopped off the table to scurry after Samson.

"I think you know what I mean," I told Gunther as I stood up and snatched the books. "Your 'I'm flirting but acting like I'm not flirting' thing." I stacked the books from my side of the table and walked them over to the bookshelf.

"Am I flirting?" Gunther asked. I could hear the amusement in his voice even though I refused to look at him.

"Are you?"

"Depends. Is the flirting working?" I blushed but continued to shelve each volume, one by one. Slowly. So I wouldn't have to turn around and look at him until the surge of pink faded from my face.

"No."

"Charlotte?"

"Yes?"

"You know your neck flushes pink when you blush, too, so turning your back to me isn't hiding anything," he told me. I hurled the books back on the shelves as fast as I could and spun around. He was laughing at me.

I did not smile back.

"Well, at least you're getting practice in for Impy," I told him with a little more snark than I intended, crossing my arms. "All those hot girls you went to school with will freak out when they find out you were actually cute under all that bright light."

"So you think I'm cute? Is that what you're saying?" Gunther asked, smiling.

"I didn't say *I* thought you were cute," I told him as Fiona stepped into my yurt. My declaration stopped her in her tracks as her eyes glanced from Gunther to me. Fiona waited for someone to say something, but Gunther only grinned at her.

With a roll of her eyes and an exhale, she spun and left the yurt without saying a word.

Traitor.

"One of these days, Charlotte, you're going to realize we should absolutely go out on a date. I'm telling you." Gunther shoved his chair away from the table.

"One of these days you're going to realize that you're a full-blooded witch now and you can date anyone you want," I told him.

"I already *do* realize that, and I still think we should at least go on one date," Gunther told me, stacking the books in front of him. "I mean, at least reject me *after* we've had a bad date. Rejecting me *before* that just seems judgmental and unfair."

I sighed.

Gunther reached for a scroll to roll it up. As he rolled, he paused and looked up at me. "You do realize I'm serious, don't you?"

"You do realize you've never actually asked me on a date, right? Besides, it doesn't matter if you're serious or not," I told him. "We're both going to be ringmasters. We can never date because we'll never see each other."

Gunther laughed.

"What? What was that for?"

"Your insistence we can never date because we will never see each other has a clear argument."

"Oh?"

"You and I see each other *every* day now. For hours at a time. In fact, I think I see you more than I see my father."

"Right, but you're not the ringmaster yet," I told Gunther as I grabbed the scrolls from the table to place them back in the cabinet.

"Let me ask you something."

"Shoot."

"Before you became ringmaster, did you live your life while you waited for a maybe? Or did you just go about your life, and live it, and adapt when your trajectory changed?"

"That's not the same thing at all, and you know it," I told him. "I had no idea at all I would become ringmaster. There was no way I could have planned for it. I didn't even really comprehend it was a possibility."

"I only know it's a *possibility* for me. Nothing is ever certain, Charlotte. My father could live for hundreds of years."

"Oh, come on, Gunther. It's more than a possibility for you, and you know it," I argued. "You're the only one of your bloodline left. Besides, you haven't visited a single paranormal town since becoming a full witch. I bet you'll meet someone perfect for you. That's easier to do when you don't glow like a light bulb, you know."

Gunther grabbed my hand and pressed it with a sigh.

"You're a headstrong woman, Charlotte Astley."

"I am not! I'm just a realist." I yanked my hand away.

I agree with Gunther, Samson said.

Shut up. No one asked you.

CHAPTER 2

SALMON.

If you don't let me concentrate, we'll never get there.

Salmon.

Samson, be quiet. Let me focus.

Salmon salmon salmon.

"Is there any way at all to make that cat shut his mouth?"

"He's not talking," Fiona said, confused.

"He is," Uncle Phil told her. "He's got that telepathic link with Charlotte and me both, and we're very clear on what he wants. He's repeating it like he's a broken record."

"What's a record?" Ningul asked as he walked up. Fiona lit up and grabbed his hand.

"It's a diary, isn't it?" Fiona told him.

"No, it's like a ledger with lines of money in it," Anya said as she walked up.

"A diary of money?" Ningul asked.

"Could all of you stop talking?" I asked them with no little exasperation. Holding my hand out, I manifested a dictionary and handed it to Ningul. "Here. Look it up in the dictionary."

"What's a dictionary?" Ningul asked as he turned the book over in his hands.

Salmon.

I glared at everyone assembled, spun on my heel, and walked away.

"Charlotte, where are you going?"

"To move the midway! Alone! In a corner! You're all driving me absolutely crazy!"

Without bothering to look back at the group, I stomped off to hide behind the roller coaster. I hoped the fake engines that fake ran the thing would act like white noise and drown out everyone, both inside and outside my head.

As I turned the corner, I smacked into Bolt, the handsome elf that kept the Sticky Walls ride spinning. His hands shot out and grabbed my shoulders before I lost my balance and tumbled into the dirt.

"Charlotte, are you all right? I'm incredibly

sorry. There's usually no one wandering around back here so I wasn't taking the care that I should," he said releasing me. "I didn't harm you, did I?"

"No, I'm okay," I told him and pulled my exploded hair back into a ponytail. My nose ached after colliding with his muscular chest. "I didn't hurt *you*, did I? I feel like I stabbed you with my nose."

"Oh, no. Hold still, Charlotte." He leaned down to peer at my face. He withdrew a clean, white rag from his back pocket and gently wiped my cheek. "I'm afraid my shirt got some oil on you." He continued to carefully rub the rag gently on my lip, and then my nose as I stared up into his ice blue-gray eyes.

"There," he said, standing back to his full 6´4˝ height. "As lovely as ever."

I blushed.

"Where were you going in such a hurry?" I asked him.

"Oh, just back to the yurt," he answered. "I'd like to clean up before we arrive at the Jamboree. You seemed to be in quite a hurry yourself."

"I was just trying to move the midway, and everyone was chattering in my ear."

It's my job to chatter in your ear. My

responsibility. And leaving the area does not get my voice out of your head, you know. I can prattle in your head from the other side of the fairgrounds.

"Now only Samson is chattering in my ear," I told Bolt. "It's not perfect, but it's better than it was before." The longer I stared at the elf, the more I felt my heart flutter inside my chest. Bolt's gaze was magnetic.

Elves have magical powers of beauty and seduction.

I believe it. Holy blue rose, he's cute. How did I not notice how cute he was when I talked to him during the whole human/council issue?

Adrenaline dims the response, and you were worried about Mark. It's a defense that all witches have against natural elven charm. When you're relaxed, though, it can be overwhelming if they turn it on.

I'm not relaxed, though.

Apparently, you're relaxed enough.

"I would be happy to escort you to a private area and keep everyone away if you need solitude, Charlotte," Bolt said, smoldering in my direction. My head suddenly felt woozy, as if I were drunk.

"I…uh, I can…that would be…"

"That's all right, I've got her," Gunther said as

he rapidly stepped up on Bolt and me. "I'm sure you were busy, elf."

"I'm *never* too busy to serve our ringmaster," Bolt told Gunther, leaning closer to me. "Service to the Magical Midway is an honor for an elf. We bring status to our clans by serving high leadership."

"Charlotte doesn't need *service*," Gunther said tightly. He reached for my arm.

"I could use…um…what was I saying?"

"Come on, Charlotte, you have to move the midway," my friend said. Gunther stepped in front of Bolt to put himself between me and the sexy elf. "People are waiting on you."

"Yeah, I have to…um…wow, I'm a little dizzy…" Gunther walked with me toward the darkness behind the roller coaster, but I twisted back toward Bolt. "Bye! Sorry again for…the bang?"

Bolt smiled at me and bowed. Gunther yanked me away.

"Ow, quit," I complained and shrugged my arm out of Gunther's hand. "Why are you being such a jerk?"

"I'm not, I'm trying to get you outside of his influence so your head will clear. Here, sit down." Gunther placed me gently on a chair at the back of the roller coaster. "Breathe in and out, deeply. You should stop feeling quite so woozy in a minute."

"I don't feel w-w-woozy," I told him and then burst into a giggle while the world tilted as if I had vertigo. Gunther knelt down in front of me and stared into my face with concern. "Gunther, you look like my dad when he's very, very unhappy with me…are you very, very unhappy with me?" I asked him. I exploded into laughter and slapped my hand on his thigh.

"I'm not unhappy with you, Charlotte," he told me, grabbing my hand and encircling it with his. "Just breathe, okay? You'll be all right in a minute or two."

"You are m-m-mad at me…you're not smiling. You know, w-w-with your eyes," I told him and stamped my foot.

"I could never be mad at you," Gunther whispered. He leaned forward and brushed the hair from my face. Tingles ran up and down my spine from his touch. I closed my eyes and pushed my face into his hand. It was soft and warm, and it made me feel more stable with the vertigo attacking my mind.

"Charlotte," Gunther whispered.

"Hmmmmmmm," I said, leaning my face into his hand.

"I need to take my hand away from your face, Charlotte, and you're leaning so much of your weight on it. I'm afraid you'll fall over."

I opened my eyes, and the pitch of the ground around me slowly righted itself. I jumped back into the chair away from Gunther's hand. And face. And kneeling body that was way too close.

"What the heck? What just happened?"

"Elves have powers of seduction, and that energy can be very intoxicating. It seems Bolt decided to turn on his attraction for you and ringmasters are not immune to their power," Gunther explained.

"Bolt *attracted* to me? Of course he's not," I told Gunther. Pushing up from the chair, I stumbled, and Gunther caught me. I shoved away as if he'd burned me, and Gunther flinched. "Anyway, I need to move this stupid circus. The sun's setting."

"It is," he agreed, stepping back into the friend zone where he needed to be. "I thought I'd come to the Jamboree with you if that's okay. I figured we could take a break and decompress from all the work we've been doing."

"Good deal," I agreed. "Just keep me away

from elves; that woozy thing could be dangerous."

"Absolutely. I can commit to that without a problem. Believe me. No problem with that at all," Gunther agreed a little too enthusiastically.

Trees appeared everywhere. In yurts. On the pathways. Up through canvas tops. It took me two hours of magical work to repair the damage I did when I plopped down the Magical Midway on top of a forest without thinking about clearing a place for it.

"I think that's it," I told Gunther after relocating the last of the most damaging trees. I wiped the sweat from my face with a towel. "That was exhausting."

"That's it, she says," Enya, a werewolf, mumbled as she walked by. Her friend, Lyndis, nodded and glared at me. "I like the forest as much as the next wolf, but not exploding through my yurt! Idiot."

"I'm sorry! At least no one was hurt, right?" I told them.

"*This* time," Lyndis snapped.

"That's enough," Gunther snapped back,

uncharacteristically annoyed at Lyndis's comment. "Give her a break, will you? Haven't you ever made a mistake?"

"That could have injured over a hundred people?" Enya asked as she kept walking past us. "Nope, can't say that I have."

Slamming down onto a bench, I watched the two wolf women walk away and tried not to take the sullen backward glances personally. They *were* right. I assumed that I could move the midway easily without Uncle Phil's guidance for a change, but I was wrong. I forgot to specify that I wanted to be put down in a clearing. The midway plopped itself down right next to the Jamboree in a thick forest of tall evergreens.

"Charlotte?"

"Just give me a minute to catch my breath, Gunther," I told him as I stretched on the bench.

"No problem. You did great fixing all that stuff. They'll get over it."

"I shouldn't have had to fix anything, and there shouldn't be anything for them to get over. That was a ridiculous mistake on my part."

"Oh, I don't know," Gunther said as he sat down next to me. "I kind of like the trees on the paths. It really gives this whole place a different feel, you know? Like you brought the forest into the fairground."

"I *did* bring the forest into the fairground. Into yurts, into beds. Anya almost throttled me when she found a big tree stuck in the middle of her king-sized water-bed."

"She'll get over it. You got it all fixed up."

The midway inhabitants shuffled toward the gate and the Werebear Jamboree. It was strange to see the carnies and paranormals walking in clusters toward *another* festival for a change. They looked just like the humans that came to see us, though they streamed in the opposite direction.

Suddenly, the low murmur of the crowd was shattered by the sound of a furious roar.

"Is that normal?" I asked Gunther. Another roar, and then another filled the air.

"I don't think so," he said, leaning forward. The stream of paranormals that had been headed toward the festival moved back toward the Magical Midway like a wave that receded from the shore. "We *are* lawgivers, maybe we need to check that out."

I nodded as Gunther grabbed my hand, and we ran toward the angry sound.

∾

Bears surrounded a tree in a half-circle. There must have been fifty or sixty crowded against one another. A man with a gray beard and glasses hung, impaled, on a branch.

He was dead.

"What happened here?" I asked as we ran into the circle. Before I reached the end of my question, the gathered bears in humanoid and shifted form fell silent and turned on me.

"Our leader is dead, *clearly*," a large man I didn't know informed me. "Who are you and what business is it of *yours*?"

"That's the witch!" a male voice yelled from the crowd.

"We're lawgivers," Gunther told him, holding up his hand to show the man the ring. "How did this man become impaled on a tree? Was there some kind of accident?"

"Have you ever heard of a *bear* accidentally becoming *impaled* on a tree, lawgiver? What kind of stupid question is that? Someone stabbed him with a branch."

"That's the other witch!" another man from the crowd hollered.

"Of course they are witches! They're lawgivers. The witches wouldn't allow that ring on any non-witch hand. I'm not an *idiot*, Fargo," the huge man snapped, and then turned back to Gunther and me. "I am Scout, and this impaled werebear is my brother Chase. We are...were the clan leaders of the Werebears."

"Your family are the leaders?" I asked.

"My brother was clan leader. Now, my brother is dead as you can plainly see," Scout said as he made his way down the embankment toward us. "I am now rightful bear clan leader. As their rightful leader, I say you have no business here!"

"Yeah, get out!" a voice called from the crowd. Growls followed.

"I mean no disrespect, sir, but we *are* lawgivers. I think we're required by our position to help with situations like these," I told Scout. "Your brother is impaled on a branch five inches thick and three feet long. That doesn't happen by accident."

"No. You are right, witch, it probably did not happen by accident. It could happen by *magic*," he growled. "Weren't you tossing around one-hundred-year-old trees like toothpicks less than an hour ago? Maybe you tossed one in the wrong direction. *Accidentally*," he said, his voice dripping with sarcasm. The surrounding men and bears nodded and closed the circle around us.

"Maybe on purpose!" another yelled from the crowd.

"She's a ringmaster, she could kill anyone she wanted!"

"And make it look like an accident!"

"Who would stop her? They don't have to follow the law like we do!"

"Charlotte, I think we should let these folks handle this on their own for now," Gunther said as he grabbed my arm. "They know where we are if they need help."

"I didn't *kill* anyone, not even accidentally!" I told them as they gathered even closer, ignoring Gunther. "I was meticulous when moving the trees. There was protection built into the relocation spell! Even for the trees themselves!"

"Clearly *not*," Scout sneered as he pointed to his brother and advanced on me. "You don't care one whit for other paranormals. It would mean nothing to you to fling a branch at my brother, accidentally or otherwise."

I stared at the large man with a thick wooden branch sticking out of his chest. He was impaled to the trunk of the tree, but it was clear that the branch thrust into the leader came from someone he was facing.

"When did you find your brother?"

"I'm not answering any of your questions, witch. And if you don't leave, I'll make sure these bears get you out," Scout growled at me.

"Charlotte, you need to go," Gunther whispered urgently.

"I can't be hurt here, Gunther," I told him and shrugged him off. "We need to figure out what happened."

"You're not *helping* here," Gunther said as he eyed the slowly advancing bears. "You need to go. Let me see if I can calm the crowd down."

"*You* can be hurt. I'm not going to leave you here!"

"I'll be fine. I'm not a ringmaster, and they don't see me as a threat. For whatever reason, at the moment, all their anger is focused on you."

I turned back to the crowd and sampled their thoughts and energy. Gunther was right. All the bears' anger, mistrust, and suspicion were focused clearly and completely on me while Gunther's presence barely registered on them. I couldn't understand why.

"Okay, okay. Meet me back at the Magical Midway."

As I gathered myself to teleport back to my yurt, a woman at the very edge of the clearing caught my eye. All around me faces were angry, grief-stricken...She looked smug as our eyes met.

I rubber-banded the half-mile back to the midway and manifested in the branches of an evergreen tree that had taken up residence in my sitting area.

Chase Trout was a significant leader to the werebears. Since he was murdered, all the bears will be out for blood.

"Samson is right. Are you absolutely sure there is no way you could have *accidentally* impaled him on that branch?" Uncle Phil asked. As he caught sight of my expression, he held up his hands. "I'm not accusing you of anything, dear girl. But accidents *do* happen, and you have been having a problem with the placement of trees today."

"Okay, I'll admit that I screwed up moving the Magical Midway to its new location. All of you talking to me and chattering at me was stressing me out," I told Uncle Phil. "While I may not have remembered to clear all the trees from where we would land, I always make *absolutely* sure to put in the safeties so that no one will be hurt. That's not something I forget."

"If she hadn't, we would've had a lot more paranormals impaled by trees," Fortuna pointed out. "At least a third of us wound up with our faces buried in needles or leaves, but no one had a scratch."

"That's true for the major move, but did you remember every single time you moved a single tree during cleanup?" Ningul asked. "I'm not accusing you of anything, either, but that was a lot of chances to make a mistake."

"I agree, but I know I didn't move that tree, and even if I did, that wasn't what killed him."

"How do you know?" Fiona asked.

"It was *huge*. The tree was one hundred feet or more. I never moved anything that big individually. Most of the trees that I moved from the Magical Midway were new growth trees. Much smaller. I think the largest one I moved may have been twenty-five feet high?"

"She's right," Gunther said as he walked in. "I was with Charlotte the whole time she was moving trees. I never saw a tree that massive."

I'm tied to you every moment of the day and night, Charlotte, Samson reminded me. *I am one hundred percent sure you did not move that tree, and you did not kill, accidentally or otherwise, Chase Trout.*

You couldn't have mentioned that before?

No one asked me.

"Samson just said that I definitely didn't kill the werebear leader."

"Yeah, well, it's not like we can hear him," Fiona said as Samson hissed at her.

"I did hear him, and Charlotte is correct," Uncle Phil said.

"That's not what I meant," Fiona said. "Oh, forget it."

"The trust you all have in me is heartwarming. Really. In any case, the branch that the leader was impaled on wasn't *from* that tree. The tree was an evergreen, and the branch was clearly oak-like. It was pinning him *to* that tree like someone flung a branch at him at high speed."

"What's the situation over there?" Uncle Phil asked Gunther, ignoring me. My face burned red.

"At the moment? Just a lot of assumptions," Gunther said. He walked around the center table and sat in a chair at the opposite end from me. "I don't know that the Forest family talked to anyone regarding the Magical Midway coming here. The circus does not seem that welcome. At least if the new leadership is any indication."

"Not wanting us here and accusing Charlotte of murder are two very different things, Gunther," Uncle Phil said. "How did she become the target of their suspicion so quickly?"

"I don't really know," Gunther answered. "Scout Trout—"

"Scout Trout?" I asked. Gunther nodded.

"The Trout family are the clan leaders of all werebears. Scout Trout is the one you met. Chase Trout, the deceased, was his older brother. In any case, Scout does not trust ringmasters, lawgivers, or the Witches' Council. Charlotte is all three, so suspicion immediately fell on her, I guess."

"You're three of those things, too," I pointed out to Gunther. "Why me and not you?"

"I'm *two* out of three," he responded. "And I didn't tussle with trees this morning."

"Well, there's nothing they can *do* to her, anyway," Fiona said as she reached out and patted my hand. "She's pretty much indestructible."

"I don't think my physical safety is the main concern in this situation," I told Fiona. "The whole point of coming here was to get the werebears on our side. Build bridges between paranormal communities, allow the town paranormals to get to know us and start tearing down the prejudices between us. The bears

thinking I *killed* their leader does exactly the
opposite of what we were trying to achieve."

"There's another complication," Gunther said
quietly. "The werebears are going to convene
their own inquiry panel in three days. If they
decide to indict Charlotte, I'm obligated as a
lawgiver to respect their decision. I'll have to
arrest her."

"That means handing me over to the Witches'
Council," I told him.

"You can't *do* that!" Fiona shouted.

"If we're going to follow the rules and laws
and we're not going to be corrupt, we might *have*
to," Gunther told her. "I don't *want* to, but to not
respect their decision would go against *everything*
Charlotte and I have been trying to champion.
We can't just bend the rules when it suits us.
That's something the Witches' Council
would do."

"She's not going to achieve anything if she's in
prison, Gunther!"

"You know, there *was* a reason we just made
our own rules," Uncle Phil told Gunther, and then
he sighed. "You children and your high ideals.
You just painted yourselves into a corner with
them."

"Look, we have three days," I told Uncle Phil.

"We know that this accusation is probably coming from the prejudice we're trying to fight against. It *has* to be. The best way to fight against it is to find out who killed Chase Trout, and why. Show the werebears we're on their side."

"That may be extremely difficult to do if the entire werebear community thinks you just *killed* Chase Trout," Gunther said.

"Yeah, well, it's not like we haven't dealt with difficult things before," I told Gunther with a shrug.

Despite my shrug, my blood pressure rose even as my heart sank.

Barely any time had passed between now and the last crisis. With each phase of the moon, my life got more and more complicated.

CHAPTER 3

I STOOD IN FRONT OF JEANNIE'S SNACK SHOP AND gazed out toward the Werebear Jamboree. Many large, powerfully built werebears gathered in clusters just outside of the Magical Midway entrance talking to one another. Many of those werebears stared at me, but no one crossed into our fairground.

None looked friendly.

"You know, there's a lake right at the bottom of the mesa," Anya said as she came up behind me. "I can suck the whole lot of those accusatory bears right down the slope with one good wave."

"You can drown a bunch of werebears with a gigantic wave coaxed out of a mountain lake, but your sister couldn't get a water snake to go fast enough to slip up my nose?"

"I'm better than my sister. Besides, there was poison in the water. The poison makes the water far harder to control. Water doesn't like to be used that way," she told me as she watched the groups of werebears at the gate.

"But it doesn't mind being turned into a gigantic wave to wash away a bunch of bears?"

"I know, seems strange, doesn't it? Alexa sends her regards, by the way."

"That's a little…weird. I would have thought your sister still hated me. How's she doing?"

"Her cell is nicer than my yurt, so she's managed to lower her rage toward you."

"That's good to know, since it looks like I may wind up in the cell right next to her."

"That *would* be an irony, wouldn't it?"

"Here you go, Charlotte," Jeannie said, sliding me a slice of wish-granted Costco pizza and a soda. "I think it's just about perfect now. It took me a while to figure out the key to it. Lots of cheese. Lots and lots of it."

I took a bite of the cheesy concoction and shuddered at the familiar greasy warmth. "Iss good, 'fank you," I told her, my mouth stuffed full of mozzarella.

"All the choices you have here, you eat that?" Anya shuddered. "You are such a creature of habit. And I don't mean that in a good way. Your habits are incredibly boring."

"Boring can be good."

"Speaking of boring," Anya pointed toward the gate. "The blond boy wonder is back." Anya's vocabulary had expanded to include many phrasings from *Batman*, an old show I had introduced her to. I had manifested a tablet so I could stay connected to some of my old, familiar guilty pleasures.

"What'd you find out?" I asked him as he walked up.

"Not much, actually," Gunther answered. "No one's really talking to me. Scout said that the inquiry will be handled the way any other werebear inquiry would be handled. He politely informed me that they no longer have any procedures to incorporate lawgivers in their investigations."

"Scout? You're on a first name basis with the new werebear leader? The same one that is accusing Charlotte of murder?" Anya asked him suspiciously.

"It's called building rapport," he told Anya. "I can't find out any information if they don't trust me. If they don't trust me, I can't help Charlotte."

"It seems to me that whenever you're around, Charlotte winds up getting in some kind of trouble."

"Yeah, but that's only because he's always around," Fortuna said as she walked up to us. "I get the feeling that Charlotte could get herself into pickles all by herself just fine."

"Why would Charlotte put herself into a pickle? How would she even shrink herself that small?" Anya asked, looking confused.

I rolled my eyes.

"Look, I can't stay here hiding for three days and just wait for them to come for me. If Gunther's not finding out anything, we need to go out and talk to people."

"Faleena!" Anya shouted at a large, round woman who waddled through the Magical Midway gate. The woman was wrapped in brown leather accented by what looked like bearskin. A werebear wearing actual bearskin seemed a little bit horrifying, to tell you the truth. "Faleena Hobb! I hoped that I would see you at this fish fest!"

"Anya, my friend," the large woman called, shuffling up to our group. "I had no idea that you were at the same circus that is headed by the ringmaster suspected of killing our leader."

With a shock, I realized she was the smug woman from the clearing.

"I didn't kill anyone," I told the woman.

"No doubt the truth of whether you did or did not matters a great deal to you. I don't believe the inquest will bother being concerned with such a piddly thing as truth," the woman responded, rolling her eyes. "Once our inquisitions turn upon someone, they *rarely* turn away."

Okay, maybe that's just her personality.

"Werebears are either remarkably talented at spotting guilty parties, or ridiculously corrupt in punishing innocent people, then," I responded. Anya laughed at my observation, but the woman's eyes narrowed in her pudgy face.

"I have no doubt it's the latter, but it's not like anyone on the Witches' Council cares one whit or another. They just take the people we hand over and deal with them in whatever way they feel they should. We don't cause them any issues."

"If it works for you," I told her, gritting my teeth.

"Well, it works for me. But then again, I'm not suspected of any crime at the moment. I imagine if I were in your position I would feel quite different about the whole thing. I suppose you think there's nothing they can really do to you, so you're probably not worried at all."

"How so?"

"Clearly you're powerful enough to avoid any consequences."

"That would make me just as corrupt as everybody else."

"When everyone is corrupt, what's one more person, more or less?" Faleena asked.

"When that person is me, it matters. I'll stand for the inquiry just like anyone else, if it comes to that. I won't be found guilty, though. I didn't do anything wrong. And I don't think it will come to that."

Faleena eyed me suspiciously, and then nodded.

"She's really quite adorable," Faleena said to Anya. "I'm surprised you haven't nailed this one down."

"She bats for another team," Anya laughed and pointed to Gunther. "That's the ball she refuses to hit, too."

Gunther blushed.

"In any case, you don't date witches, Faleena," Anya said.

"Right, right. But really, I'll try anything once.

Sometimes twice, if it's fun."

"Dated any more naiads lately?"

"Oh no, my dear skinhead sprite," Faleena shook her head no and laughed. "You were definitely an experience that I would be unable to repeat."

"You and she were an item?" Gunther asked, surprised. Fortuna elbowed him in the ribs.

"No, actually," Anya asked him, turning toward Faleena. "I was talking about my sister, Alexa."

"Right, right! My memory isn't what it used to be," Faleena told Anya, slapping her arm. "You and your sisters are so similar it's hard not to get one of you confused with the other."

I stared at Faleena. The naiad sisters were actually distinctly different from one another. Someone getting the long-haired, quiet Alessandra mixed up with bald, boisterous Anya or the garish, conniving Alexa was not something I could see.

"I just didn't know that…um…naiads and bear shifters dated," Gunther said as the women stared at him.

"Yes, I'm sure *that's* what you didn't know," Faleena said, and Gunther blushed an even deeper red.

"I want to go talk to Scout," I told Gunther.

"Not a chance."

"I would be happy to escort you both to the wake circle," Faleena said with a little too much eagerness. "It will be taking place for the first day of the Jamboree so that people can pay their respects."

"I don't think that's a good idea," Gunther said.

"We need to learn more about Chase and Scout. What better way to do it than by showing up at the funeral? Besides, if I don't pay my respects, it's going to look suspicious."

"Yes, I agree with her. She's critical, and she *must* pay our leader her respects. Even if she murdered him, that would be expected," Faleena agreed.

Faleena sent Anya off, informing her she wasn't nearly important enough to attend the vigil. Anya shrugged and left the three of us alone.

"Are we ready?"

"I'm still not comfortable with this," Gunther said as we walked.

"You are a very nervous little man, aren't you, Mr. Makepeace?"

Gunther stopped walking and stared at her. "*Excuse* me?"

"Such concern you have for an omnipotent being," Faleena pointed out. Gunther stared at the werebear, and I could see the red flush of anger creeping up his neck. I expected friends of Anya to be a little rough-and-tumble, but Faleena took it to a whole new level.

"I would not enter anyone's fire circle,." Faleena grabbed my arm before I crossed a makeshift entry point. "You are certainly not welcome at most firesides. If you try, you will wind up provoking whatever family or tribe controls the area. Their honor will demand that they eject you. Forcefully. So you should stay away from everyone if you can."

"Have you heard anything further about what happened to Chase Trout?"

"No doubt when we get to where his body is on display, there will be people assembled there discussing the situation. I have to warn you, Ms. Astley, your presence will *not* be welcome. This festival has turned from a celebration into a gathering of mourners, and an angry one at that."

"I understand," I told her.

"Just through these trees over here," Faleena pointed to a pathway lined with softly glowing candles. As we continued slowly up the route, I heard the echoes of arguing and weeping.

"Are you sure you wish to do this, Ms. Astley? Mr. Makepeace?"

"I can't sit on my hands and do nothing, Faleena. And please, call me Charlotte. If you keep calling me Ms. Astley, I'm going to keep feeling like a suspect in a murder investigation."

"As well you should, since you are," she responded coldly. I glanced sharply at Anya's friend, but she didn't return the look.

We came through the trees, and Faleena stopped short. "Well, this just got more entertaining," she whispered under her breath.

"What?"

"Wayland is here."

Gunther cursed.

As we walked in, silence descended abruptly, cutting off the conversations and expressions of grief. The clearing held at least seventy-five people, but it felt as if not a single one breathed once they noticed us. All heads turned to stare.

We stared back waiting.

After several minutes, a large, muscled man stood up and cleared his throat. His hair was white, and his beard matched the snowy fluff on his head. A considerable belly peeked out beneath his black T-shirt emblazoned with *Tough Enough to be a Blacksmith*. One large eye right in the middle of his forehead stared at me.

"Heir. Heat Merchant." The man nodded as he greeted us.

The crowd remained silent.

"What's he mean, heat merchant?" I asked Gunther quietly.

"He won't greet you as a ringmaster because you're not his ringmaster, my father is. His calling you a heat merchant was sarcastic. Basically, he's saying you attract problems."

"Wait, he's from the Makepeace Circus? Who is he?"

"Wayland Black, Chase Trout's closest friend. He's a blacksmith, and a cyclops, as well as the unofficial lay leader of our carnival."

"That I am." The man thrust his shoulders back and his chest forward. "You don't belong here, witch. Either of you."

Welcoming bunch.

"We came to pay our respects to Chase Trout,

as it's proper for us to do," I told him, and the area exploded into gasps, chatter, and shouts.

"Go home, murderer!" someone shouted from the back.

"Killer!" someone else called.

"Everybody shut up!" At Wayland's loud demand, the grove's deafening chatter grew quiet, then silent. "Let the murderer and her entourage say what they have to say. We're waitin'."

A cyclops raising his only eyebrow at me was a frightening sight. Just as I prepared to speak, a shout cut me off.

"We don't answer to outsiders, and we sure don't listen to them anymore. You are *not* one of us, either," Scout Trout told Wayland. He pushed his way into the clearing and made his way aggressively toward the huge man.

"Your brother never considered me an outsider, kid," Wayland said leaning into the new leader of the werebears. "I'm certainly not going to let some young upstart push me out of my best friend's wake."

"Blood ties last beyond death. Unless you've been visited by my brother's ghost? You are *nothing* to him anymore. And without him, cyclops, you are nothing to *us*."

"Your brother always said you were the stupid

one," Wayland sneered, and then he spat on the ground. Reaching into his back pocket, he pulled out a parchment and waved it in Scout's face. "Your brother made me the executor of his estate upon his death. You got no legal standing to keep me out of here."

"He's dead. The paper is meaningless."

"*Because* he's dead, the paper is binding," Wayland shot back. "And until your brother is in the ground three days hence, you're not the leader here. *I* am. It says so right here."

"You're *not* a werebear!" Scout roared. The werebears that were gathered in clusters around the clearing froze, staring at the two men challenging one another.

"He was, of course," Bolt said as he entered into the clearing to a surge of energy. As soon as Scout's eyes met Bolt's, the werebear brother's tense shoulders relaxed, and his angry face smoothed into a placidly calm frown. "Several years ago, your brother made him an honorary member of the clan. I understand all of the Makepeace Circus members witnessed this event. Did they not?"

"We did," Gunther stated, and Wayland nodded. Scout glared at Gunther with barely contained fury.

"How did he know that?" I whispered to Gunther, and a wave of woozy vertigo washed over me. My hands and face tingled as if energy was being sprinkled all over me. Gunther grabbed me around the waist and glared at Bolt.

"My, my, isn't this an interesting drama," Faleena murmured. Bolt's eyes flickered to Faleena and then back to Scout. "Everyone is so angry and mistrustful. *Delightful.*"

Bolt continued and pushed himself to the front of the crowd.

"I propose that three days delay to your new throne, bear, is not that much of a postponement. It will give you some time to mourn your dear brother and his untimely, unexpected death."

"His *murder...*" Scout corrected.

"Yes, yes, of course. We must call things what they are, and clearly, your brother had enemies who wished him dead. Some of whom may be in this very clearing," Bolt agreed and stepped closer to the now-calm aspiring werebear leader. "As an elf, I stand ready to assist our werebear brothers and sisters in any way possible during this tragic time. We do, after all, have some useful skills at our disposal."

"We do have lawgivers here," Faleena pointed out as she gestured to Gunther and me. "They *should* be doing the inquiry, shouldn't they? The Witches' Council hasn't disbanded them. Well, not yet."

"Not when one is suspected of the murder, and the other has a history of protecting the one suspected," Bolt disagreed. "Forgive my insinuation, Ringmaster, but we must ensure that the inquiry is above reproach."

"Of course, elf. That seems wise," Faleena said, publicly ensuring that Gunther and I would have a difficult time with any investigation. Did she speak up for us to *get* us in the investigation or to get us *out* of it?

Because if it was the latter, well done.

"You're a member of the Magical Midway. How is *your* assistance supposed to be above reproach?" Wayland asked.

"Elves are well known to cleave to the law," Scout told Wayland. "His loyalty is to the highest law in the land based on the elven code. He's fine. Better than you."

"Anything is better than those two witches!" someone shouted from the crowd.

"I hand this over to you, Bolt, and put you in charge of the inquiry into my brother's murder," Scout said. Bolt nodded and bowed to the next werebear leader.

"You're *not in charge here,*" Wayland growled at him.

"Then do your own damn inquiry!" Scout snapped at him. Bolt placed a hand on Scout's shoulder, and he relaxed. "I just want to ensure my brother's murderer is brought to justice. I welcome additional investigations. Please do your own."

"You bet I will," Wayland told him, turned, and left the clearing.

"What does Bolt have to do with all this?" I asked Gunther once we returned to my yurt.

"Elves are always getting involved in things that they shouldn't be," Faleena told me as she followed us in. "The paranormal world would be far less dramatic if those shiny white busybodies just minded their own business."

"About a month ago, Bolt helped Fiona and me with some information. He was perfectly charming and incredibly useful to talk to."

"Of *course* he was," Faleena rolled her eyes, as Uncle Phil entered the yurt with Samson. "Elves can be incredibly charming. Especially when they want something from you."

"But he didn't want anything from me. I wanted something from him."

"That's what you think. Elves always have an agenda. Even if you think it's your agenda, by the end of dealing with them, you might find out it was never yours at all."

"Clearly, he has a vested interest in what's going on here. I'm curious, Charlotte—was Bolt the one that suggested the Magical Midway come to the Werebear Jamboree?" Gunther asked.

"No. He didn't talk to me about the Werebear Jamboree at all. Aldo Forest visited me during open office hours and suggested that we come. He thought it would be a good opportunity for the werebear community to get to know us, and for the cubs to experience a circus."

Faleena Hobb stared at me, her eyes narrowing.

"What?"

"We don't call our children *cubs*."

"What do you call them?"

"Children."

"Right, sorry," I told her.

I'm sorry about that, Samson said. *The children have always been called cubs as far as I can remember.*

They have, Uncle Phil agreed. *Not calling them*

cubs seems to be a new thing. I wonder where that came from.

"Are we done with the discussion yet?" Anya stomped into my yurt. "This is a festival, and I have friends I'd like to go visit. I need Faleena."

"You are as impatient as you ever were," the werebear responded. "I would think a murder investigation imperiling your friend would trump your need for socialization."

"If my sister couldn't kill her, I highly doubt that anyone else could," Anya scoffed. "She'll be fine."

"Your sister thought she could do it on her own using the aid of two idiot werelions. I highly suggest that you stick to the side of your ringmaster like glue. No offense. And if the framing now includes an elf, she may wish to take this a little more seriously."

"Framing? Wait a minute, who said anything about me being framed?" I asked Faleena. "So far, this just looks like a run-of-the-mill accusation based on prejudice and intolerance."

"You're very naïve, aren't you?" Faleena raised her eyebrow. "Anya, I insist we remain with Ms. Astley as much as possible. Clearly, she needs our aid."

"I'm not going to make a bunch of

assumptions based on one conversation in the forest. Seriously, we'll be fine. You guys go say hi to whoever. If we need you, we'll find you."

A flash of frustration exploded out of Faleena, and then it was gone. I couldn't understand why this woman I just met was so concerned about me, but I didn't want to ruin the festival for Anya. She really needed a party after all that stuff with her sister.

"Talk to your Aldo Forest," Faleena snapped her fingers. "I would bet a week's worth of salmon that the idea to bring the Magical Midway here was not his own."

Take the bet. Please take the bet.

Samson, you really need to focus on the fact that a murder took place. You aren't getting any salmon until we figure out who killed Chase Trout and why.

That's cruel and unusual punishment, Charlotte. And not something you can enforce anyway. I can catch my own dang fish, thank you very much.

"What are you two going to do?" I asked Anya.

"I am going to go say hello to all of my old friends at the festival," she said. "I'll get them all drunk, and see what they say. Faleena and I will report back to you in the morning. See? I can have fun and help at the same time. I'm very good at doing two things at once."

CHAPTER 4

"Tell me about Wayland," I asked Gunther the next morning while we sat in my yurt and drank coffee. "Has he been with the Makepeace Circus long?"

"All my life," Gunther responded. "He's a cyclops, so he's a rough-and-tumble kind of guy. Long-lived. I've never known him not to be honorable, though, even though he's kind of a jerk. Chase Trout was like a brother to him. Years ago, the werebear saved Wayland's sister from being drowned by a bloodthirsty mob. He risked his life for her even though he didn't know her. Since then, Wayland felt like he owed him."

"I guess so," I nodded. "How long ago was this?"

"It had to be more than a hundred years ago," Gunther stared into his coffee thinking. "I suppose it could have been more than that. Time is funny in the paranormal world. Lifespans can be so long, and you just don't notice it."

"Can I ask you something?"

"Shoot," Gunther smiled and leaned forward.

"How come you haven't used one of the lawgiver guilty-person powers on me?" Gunther's smile faded from his face. "I mean, you're just *assuming* I didn't kill Chase Trout. You have the ability to confirm it for yourself, you know."

"Of course you didn't."

"But a lot of people seem to think I did. Don't you want to make *sure*?"

"You're ridiculous, Charlotte." Gunther put his coffee cup down. "I know you didn't kill the bear. I don't think you're capable of taking a branch and thrusting it through a person. I don't need to tell you to freeze and see if you do. Besides, though, you're a witch. Our lawgiver powers don't work on witches. Just other paranormals."

Yet again I find the Witches' Council concerned with everybody else other than themselves.

"You wanted to see me, Charlotte?" Aldo Forest stuck his head in my yurt and waited to be invited in. I waved the massive werebear into the room and motioned to one of the chairs sitting around the table.

"Obviously, you've heard about what's been going on," I told Aldo once he took a seat across from Gunther and me. "First, I want to offer my deepest sympathies on the loss of your werebear leader. I didn't know Chase Trout at all, but I'm really sorry I never got to."

"I appreciate that, Charlotte, thank you," Aldo said, nodding. "I think you would've liked him. He was a good and fair leader, always protecting the werebear community from the Witches' Council if he had the ability to do so. I think you and he would have had much to talk about, and he would've supported your seat and your agenda both."

"Once things calm down, I think Scout will as well. I'm sure he'll make a fine leader for the werebears."

Aldo sat quietly and stared at me. He looked deep into my eyes, the silence was punctuated by the rustling of denim, as the big man shifted in his seat from one side to another. As if he suddenly came to a decision, Aldo nodded to himself and began to speak.

"I wouldn't be so sure about that, ma'am,"

Aldo said, a dark look passing over his hairy face. "Scout has never been even half the bear that Chase was, and only a quarter of the man. It wouldn't surprise me at all if that arrogant sod had something to do with his brother's death."

"That's a *serious* accusation, Aldo," Gunther said leaning forward.

"I *am* aware, Mr. Makepeace. My words are not spoken lightly, and it gives me no pleasure to say those words out loud to outsiders. I would not say it if Scout had already been elevated to leader, as it would be a betrayal of my leader and could mean my death. But he is *not* leader, and so I can still speak my truth. For another three days, in any case."

"Do you think that's why Chase designated Wayland as his executor? Because he suspected that his brother would try to push him out of the way for some reason?"

"It would not surprise me if that were so," Aldo told me. "Our departed leader's choice has given us three days to uncover who has betrayed our community so egregiously. We have three days to speak freely, to speak frankly, and to say what we have seen and heard, without being concerned about repercussions. Once Scout is our leader, that window of truth will close, and we will owe him our allegiance."

"Just because Chase designated Wayland as executor doesn't mean Scout killed his brother," Gunther pointed out.

"I do think it means Chase thought his brother could be *capable* of it in the right circumstances," I told him. "I can't think of another reason why he would give someone outside the werebear community control of it for three full days."

"It has never been done before," Aldo told me.

"We appreciate the information and the trust you've shown us, Aldo, in sharing it. Especially considering some of the rumors about me. I do have one more question for you, though. When you asked me to bring the Magical Midway to the Werebear Jamboree, was that *your* idea?"

"I wish I could say that it was, but alas, it was young Bolt from the Sticky Walls ride. He and I met for elixirs one night, and somehow we got on the subject of the Werebear Jamboree. It was he who came up with the idea, and I thought it was a good one."

· · ·

"Did you and Bolt often meet for drinks?"
Gunther asked him.

"No, Mr. Makepeace. In fact, that was the first time."

"I *don't* want you to meet with him alone,"
Gunther insisted after Aldo left. Red splotchy patches colored my friend's face as he paced slowly around the seating area. He refused to meet my eyes.

"I didn't say I wanted to *meet* with him alone, just that I wanted to meet with him. What's got into you?"

"The last two times you were around him, he did his elf glamour garbage on you, and that's dangerous. It's not safe for you to be anywhere near him right now, Charlotte."

"You're ridiculous, witch," Faleena said. She and Anya tumbled into my yurt without bothering to wait for me to ask them in. "Bolt is a member of her circus, you jealous moron. He would never do anything to hurt her. Isn't that some big sin in *your* world?"

"I've known Bolt for years," Anya agreed. "He's

a bit boring, but he wouldn't do anything to hurt Charlotte."

"You didn't see what I saw, either of you." Gunther turned to face the women. "The night Charlotte moved the midway here, Bolt turned his full glamour power on her. It was so strong that she was dizzy for a good *five minutes* after he left."

"That doesn't sound to me like the elf wants to *hurt* her, Blondie," Faleena snickered. She walked over to my cabinet and rummaged through the human wine collection I stored there.

"Please, feel free to help yourself," I told her.

"Thanks, Charlotte, don't mind if I do," the werebear answered brightly. She grabbed a decanter and continued. "Like I was saying, Makepeace, it sounds like you've got your jodhpurs in a twist because you have some handsome, charming competition, that's all. Get over it."

"Competition for what?" I asked her.

"Are you kidding me?" Faleena asked me in response, staring at me as if I'd grown another head. Turning to Anya, she handed the naiad a drink. "Your friend is *completely* oblivious, Anya. I thought you liked them smarter than that."

"Charlotte's not dumb. She just makes sure

her focus is on much more important things. Like any powerful woman."

"Does anyone here realize that in three days time I may be accused of murder? I hate to rain on everyone's happy hour by focusing on other things, but the clock may be ticking on my freedom here. Can you let me get back to finding out who killed Chase, please?"

"Let me go talk to Bolt as a lawgiver, Charlotte," Gunther said.

"What the heck, Makepeace?" Anya whirled on Gunther. "You already trying to push Charlotte out of the role she was actually *given first*? If I remember correctly, her uncle *gave her* the lawgiver ring. You just snatched it off a dinner table and *took* it for yourself. Maybe Faleena was right about you."

"Isn't that just like a man?" Faleena laughed, and Anya and Faleena clinked glasses in agreement. "I told you, he's just trying to weasel into her position. Well, probably multiple positions..."

"Hey, watch it," I snapped.

"Apologies, Charlotte," Faleena said, laughing.

"I don't need you to talk to one of my own, Gunther. I'm happy to bring you with me if you want, but I'm not going to avoid Bolt."

"I don't trust him," Gunther disagreed.

"Why should she care if *you* trust him, Makepeace?" Faleena pointed out. "*She* trusts him. And he's a member of her circus. You're acting like a bit of a controlling twit if you ask me."

"*No one* asked you," Gunther responded in a low, harsh voice I had never heard from him before.

"Why do you even need to go with her? Please, explain to me why the woman cannot handle herself," Faleena smiled. Gunther ignored her.

"Actually, Charlotte, why are you even going to talk to Bolt? What does he have to do with the Werebear Jamboree?" Anya asked, confused. "He wasn't even here when Chase was murdered."

"How do you know that?"

"The autopsy was done," Anya said, gesturing toward Faleena.

"The murder took place right around the time the Magical Midway arrived. Unless Bolt can teleport, he wouldn't have had time to make it over to where Chase was murdered," Faleena said.

"Can elves teleport?" I asked.

"No, elves can't *teleport*," Anya told me, rolling her eyes. "When have you ever heard of a teleporting elf?"

"Bolt was the one that suggested the Magical Midway come to the Werebear Jamboree. Well, he suggested the idea to Aldo, and then Aldo brought it to me."

"What does that matter?" Faleena sat down on my couch and made herself at home.

"It may not," I told her. "It does seem strange, though. I just want to know how he came up with the idea. That's all."

"I want to know why he showed up at the scene of the murder," Gunther added. "He insinuated himself awfully quick into the investigation. He knew *right* where to be to make the assertions he did, and what to say so Charlotte and I wouldn't be trusted to investigate."

"You're *seriously* paranoid," Faleena said and waved in Gunther's direction like she was swatting a fly. "It's a festival. People wander around. He probably heard the argument and just wandered in."

"To a *wake*? How does someone just wander into a wake?" Gunther asked her.

"It could happen," Anya said thoughtfully. "I wandered into a Bear Mitzvah once."

I stared at her.

"What? You've never heard of a Bear

Mitzvah?"

"Clearly, you are both terrible at this," Faleena said, pointing to Gunther and me. "While you're arguing over who should or shouldn't talk to the dazzling elf man, neither of you have brought up the person with the most to gain."

"Who?" I glanced at Gunther, who was gritting his teeth.

"Your cyclops. Maybe this is a cyclops attack on the werebear fortunes. Or on our lands. That man could take anything we have over the next three days," Faleena admonished us as if we were children. "If I were a lawgiver, I would be looking at the person that's *already* profited from Chase's death. His 'friend' Wayland."

Once Anya and Faleena left the yurt, Gunther and I stared at each other in sullen silence. He was clearly aggravated about Bolt, and with Faleena's insinuations about Wayland. I was frustrated by... actually, everything.

This was supposed to be my vacation.

This was *not* a vacation.

"Stop, both of you," Fortuna said, sticking her head in my yurt. "I'm going to ask permission to come in but honestly, Charlotte, if you don't give it to me, I'm coming in anyway."

"Come on in," I told her without taking my eyes from Gunther. "What's up?"

"What's up is you are both broadcasting your displeasure through a mind megaphone that's bouncing like two ping pong balls on the inside of my skull," she said stepping between us. "What's wrong with you two?"

We both spoke at once.

"He doesn't trust me—"

"She won't listen to me—"

Fortuna placed her small hands over her ears and closed her eyes, while Gunther and I verbalized our annoyances simultaneously. As we spit words over one another, and Fortuna continued to guard her ears, our volume slowly lowered and our protestations trailed off.

When the silence reached beneath her hands, she peeled them away and peeked out. Smiling, her posture relaxed, and she grinned at us.

"Awesome. Now that you got that out, and you realize how silly you both sounded, let's talk."

"Why bother when you can just read our minds," I grumbled.

"That's not *my* fault," Fortuna smiled and

thumped her chest. "In fact, I think it's *your* fault if you really stop and think about it."

Gunther and I sat down with Fortuna and shared what had happened that she didn't know about, and the thoughts we had about our next move.

"What you're saying feels like the right path," she said. "You're still missing pieces, but I think you know that."

"We haven't gotten very far," I admitted.

"I can tell you that Gunther's right about Bolt," Fortuna said, lowering her voice. Her eyes darted to the door, and she leaned in. "He's hiding something deliberately within his mind. Elves can glamour their thoughts the same way that they can glamour others, sort of. When I passed by him an hour ago, it was like a white energy wave rolled over me, and I got dizzy."

"Are you okay?" Gunther asked. Fortuna waved off his concern.

"It was nothing I couldn't handle, and I don't think it was directed *at* me. I think it was sent out to obfuscate what he was thinking. I know a little about what elves can do, though, and doing something like that?" Fortuna leaned back. "It's not without effort. I can't read anything from him."

"What about Wayland?"

"Oh, Charlotte, that poor man." Fortuna's eyes teared up. "He loved his friend so much, and he's in so much pain right now over his loss. I can't believe there's *any* way that Wayland harmed Chase Trout, much less murdered him."

"Any guilt? Could it have been an accident?"

"No," Fortuna nodded. "He's also *furious* at whoever did this."

"Well, that's good, at least," I told Gunther. "Faleena seemed convinced that we should look at him. I think he'd be good to talk to, but it sounds like he's not likely a suspect."

"If there's anyone else you want me to take a peek in, let me know," Fortuna offered.

"I think we need to talk to some of these folks, first. Bolt and Wayland definitely seem like the best place to start, though I think we should start with Wayland, not Bolt," I told them.

"Why?" Gunther asked with relief.

"We don't know enough about Chase Trout right now, and I highly doubt Scout will talk to us at all anymore. I don't know who you should head-peek. Maybe just keep your mind open, if it's not too much trouble?"

"Will do, boss," Fortuna saluted and smiled.

"Don't do that," I told her.

"Sorry, boss," she said and thumped her chest like the lares guards. I imagined whacking her in the head, and she flinched.

"Ow."

"I'm going to run over to the cauldron and call my father before we go," Gunther said, standing up. "I just want to give him an overview of what's happening, especially since it involves Wayland."

"Okay, we'll be here."

"It amazes me sometimes how hard you are on him," Fortuna told me as soon as Gunther left the yurt.

"What are you talking about?"

"Charlotte, I know that you know how he feels about you," Fortuna said, placing her hand on my knee.

"I have some telepathic stuff, too, you know. I know what you're doing with your hand on my knee, Fortuna."

"I can sense the truth of how you both feel for each other. I can't help that. I've done too many readings in my life to not poke my nose in and give you advice. What I haven't been able to figure out is why you are pushing him away so hard. You have feelings for him, Charlotte. But you pretend that you don't. Why?"

"I don't want to talk about this," I told her, getting up and straightening my spotless yurt.

"See? This is exactly what I'm talking about."

I took a deep breath.

"We can never be together. Never. Entertaining any feelings that I may or may not have for that man is pointless, when you realize that our lives will never be able to intertwine," I told her without stopping my nervous cleaning.

"Ever since you became ringmaster, Charlotte, you have been so sure of so many things. Many of those things turned out not to be *quite* as you thought they were. As you got new information, you changed your perspective. You changed your view of what was possible. I mean, I'm living proof of that."

I turned around and stared at Fortuna.

"This is different."

"I don't think it is."

"There's no new information, Fortuna. No new indication that anything is changed from when my parents warned me for the first time not to become involved with him."

"Your *feelings* have changed, Charlotte!"

"That's not facts. That's not new information. That's just a…a complication."

You are such a stubborn person, Samson said as he waddled into my yurt. The cat's stomach was distended, and it swung back and forth as he walked.

"What on earth happened to you? Are you sick?"

Salmon. Lots of salmon. Amazing, succulent, juicy salmon. Werebears don't see many cats, and every fireside I visited shared their bounty with me. My belly is full of salmon.

"Your belly looks like it's about to explode," I told him as he plopped down on his side in the center of the room. "You're just going to lay in the middle of the floor?"

Can't jump. Too heavy. Can't make it to the bed. Drunk on salmon.

"Oh, for heaven's sake." I grabbed the cat and deposited him on the bed. "Better?"

Yes. Must rest. Must digest salmon. Must make room for more salmon.

"Some guardian you are, Samson."

You're not dead at the moment, are you?

"Is that your litmus test for guardian success? Is the person I'm supposed to guard breathing? If yes, time for a salmon break?"

Stop talking. Must sleep.

"It looks to me like your super magical guardian protector is going to just be a cat for today," Fortuna laughed.

"Hey, have you seen Fiona, by the way? I haven't talked to her in a while."

"I think Ningul has her in the centaur village. She apparently did not react well to the accusations against you, and he felt it was better to keep her away from the Werebear Jamboree until she calmed down."

"So, we probably won't see her until we leave, then? Or until I'm arrested, I guess."

"Charlotte, you're changing the subject. We never finished our conversation about Gunther."

"There's a reason for that. We don't need to have a conversation about Gunther."

Fortuna crossed her legs and her arms while raising her eyebrow. I didn't know how such a short, pixie-like woman could pull off such an intensely judgmental expression, but Fortuna was definitely coming into her own as a witch. Gone was the shy human just happy to be let into the paranormal party.

"Look, here's the thing," I said as I sat down next to her. "Whatever feelings I have for Gunther? They don't matter. Gunther spent his entire life being the half-human witch that was picked on and ostracized by the witch community."

"What does that have to do with anything?"

"He never had a *chance* to find a partner. I would guess, anyway. Would you date someone that you had to wear sunglasses to look at? Or who constantly advertised that they were something most people didn't approve of?"

"Well, *I* probably would, but I've always been a bit eccentric. I see a little bit of what you mean, Charlotte, but I don't think Gunther's feelings for you are simply because you're the first female to be kind to him. They run deeper than that."

"That's not something you should be telling me," I said as I turned away from her. "We all have a right to privacy."

"This is the paranormal community, Charlotte. No one expects privacy here. There's always a bit of magic or a nearby telepath to expose people's deepest, darkest secrets."

"You would think people would stop killing each other considering that little fact. And yet they don't."

Fortuna's eyes widened, and she tilted her head.

"They don't, do they?" Fortuna agreed. "But

why would you do that at a festival where so many people are in such close proximity to each other? There are more telepaths here than just you and I. Doing something like this *here*? You're almost guaranteed to be discovered. *Someone* would hear the crime in your mind."

"Unless you could block a telepath."

"Only two types of paranormals can do that, Charlotte. Elves…"

"And witches."

Great, you figured it out. Could you both stop talking and let me sleep now?

You're really failing as my familiar, Samson.

Guardian. I'm failing as your guardian. And like I said, you're still breathing, so shut up and let me get some sleep. If someone tries to kill you, give me a shout. You know where to find me.

CHAPTER 5

GUNTHER AND I WALKED ALL OVER THE WEREBEAR Jamboree for two hours, but no matter where we looked, Wayland was nowhere to be found. After asking at campsite after campsite and being lucky to get any answer at all from the angry festival goers, I was growing frustrated.

"I'm getting hungry," I told Gunther. It was almost lunchtime, and despite the shade from the tree canopy, the air felt sticky in the summer heat. I needed my magical air conditioning.

"Let's head back to your house and grab some food. We can start again after lunch."

As we walked into the living room of my yurt, I screamed.

Wayland's face glowed red from the firelight. Fire? This guy I didn't know came into my yurt and built a *fire in the fireplace* in the *middle of summer?*

With security like the Larry brothers, I didn't actually need conspiracies to put my life in peril.

"Girly, you seem a little jumpy for a ringmaster." Wayland sipped a sparkling can of… something alcoholic, judging by the smell that hit me from across the room. "I thought ringmasters were supposed to be the steady hand that steered all the rest of us away from the rocks. Or some bull like that."

"I wasn't expecting anyone to be in here since no one is *supposed* to be in here without my having invited them," I told the confident cyclops as I walked in.

"Your magic isn't worth much, then, is it?" Wayland burped. "Haven't you heard of wards?"

Glancing to look back at Gunther, I was surprised when he said nothing to Wayland. Considering they knew each other, I would have thought Gunther would at least say hello.

I turned back to the somewhat relaxed

Wayland. "We trust each other at the Magical Midway, so we don't need them."

We trust each other? Since when?

Right now I don't even trust you. How come you didn't tell me he was here?

He's not mumbling about killing you. Besides, he made it toasty warm in here, and I wanted it to last a little longer.

Stupid cat.

"Anyway, why are you in my house?"

"I heard you were looking for me. I knew that you two would be coming back here, and frankly, *I* wanted to ask some questions. Privately. As you no doubt want to ask me as well." The rotund man slammed the can he was drinking on the coffee table with a clunk and leaned forward.

"Okay, shoot."

"Why are you really here, girly? I mean, *really* here? And don't give me the same bull song and dance your bears told Chase," he snapped.

"*Don't* talk to Charlotte that way. She came here for no other reason than the reason she said. She just wanted to get to know the community and have the werebear community get to know her. She didn't do anything to your friend." Gunther stepped forward.

"Boy, you *ain't* the ringmaster here. Don't you

give me an order as if you are. *Daddy* ain't here to help you."

Wayland stood up

If that statement was designed to tick Gunther off, it worked.

The two men stared at one another across the room, muscles flexing and testosterone raging. I cast my eyes between them and worried. Sure, everyone was a little bit testy, but what on earth had been said between them that caused a reaction like this?

Gunther was only about six feet tall while Wayland had at least another foot on him. The cyclops was all hard muscle covered in blubbery fat, making a potential punch from him devastating, considering the weight he could put behind it. Gunther was muscular but lithe, so maybe he was fast enough to avoid the big man's strike, should it come to that.

With the looks on both of their faces turning to fury so quickly, I was not *entirely* sure at this point it *wouldn't* come to that. I interjected myself back into their silent confrontation.

"Guys, I realize this is a highly emotional time, and everyone is really on edge, but the two of you fighting isn't going to help anyone."

Wayland turned his single eye toward me, and I smiled.

"Just an observation."

"Girly, right now I only know two things. One is that my friend Chase is dead. Two is that everybody walkin' this festival seems to think that *you* did it. I don't know the truth of nothin', but what I do know is the son of my ringmaster is standing next to the person accused of murdering my best friend."

"You and I have had our issues, Wayland, but I'm telling you Charlotte didn't kill Chase." Gunther's fists balled against his hips and his face grew red and splotchy as he struggled to contain his anger. "She doesn't have a cruel bone in her body. Unlike you."

I stepped back.

"Yeah, whatever, boy. You believe whatever you want to believe about your little girlfriend and me over there. I don't know her from a hole in the ground. I do know that since she showed up, we've had nothing but problems and nothing but trouble."

The cyclops sneered at me as he gulped his drink again. The words and accusations coming out of his mouth would indicate that he *could* be a suspect in his friend's murder, and was just attacking to throw off suspicion. He was angry, and there was apparently something else going on here.

I stretched my senses out cautiously to get a measure of him with my intuition. His thoughts and emotions, though, confirmed what Fortuna had told me. This man was grieving. It might be tough guy mourning, but it was fueled by deep pain and regret over Chase's loss all the same.

"You asked me why I was here. My original explanation was absolutely the truth. Now I'm here to make sure that your friend's murderer is caught. I know it's not me. Granted, I don't want to go to jail for something that I didn't do, but more than that, I don't want to see someone get away with murder."

"Just words, little girl. You seem to forget something. You got *no* power here," Wayland said as he pointed his fat finger at me.

"I have more power than you think," I bragged to the big man with total confidence. Confidence that was a lie.

Wayland was more right than I was. The accusations against me had hamstrung all my lawgiver powers, and my ringmaster powers only functioned fully on the grounds of the Magical Midway. That limitation was no secret, and whoever killed Chase would likely know that.

"To keep yourself from getting stomped like a squeeze doll prize, sure. But not for much else. If you really are here to save us like some great witch savior or something, save your effort. I'll deal with it. I always do. I got a plan." Wayland's one eye fixed itself on Gunther as the big man's chubby face sneered through his beard. "I don't need *you*."

"What kind of plan?" I asked.

Wayland stared at me with his one eye and crossed his arms.

"Wayland, come on," Gunther said. "We're trying to help."

Silence.

"Who are you staying with while you're here, Wayland?" I asked.

"Not that it's any of your business, but I'm staying in Chase's cabin. He invited me to come and bunk with him, and that's where I'm staying."

"I bet that's gone over with Scout really well," I murmured to Gunther.

"I don't care *what* goes over with that kid," Wayland sneered. "I'm warning you both, though. Stay out of my way. I owe my friend, and I'll run right over both of you if you interfere."

"If you tell us what you're planning, we'd be much less likely to interfere."

"Ha. Nice try, girly. You're a slick one."

Throwing his empty cup on the floor, he stomped out of my yurt.

Once Wayland left, I prepared two sandwiches while Gunther extinguished the fire turning my yurt into a sauna.

"What was the deal with the fire?"

"Cyclops blacksmiths love heat," he answered as he poked around the remnants of the fire to ensure all the embers were cool. "I think he keeps his cabin at one hundred and twenty degrees year round. It certainly helps to keep any meetings with him short and to the point. I think this is out."

"He's not going to be any help at all, is he?" I asked as I grabbed the plates and headed toward the table.

"Wayland sober and calm can be a tough nut to crack," Gunther replied. "Now? Probably not."

With a hand wave and a surge of energy, Gunther blew a cool breeze through the tent to clear the remaining oven-like air. The temperature dropped at least twenty degrees by the time Gunther's hand fell back to his side.

"That would have been really useful to know during Texas summers," I told him as I handed him a plate.

"You had the ability all along. I'm really surprised your parents didn't teach you *some* of the basic survival stuff," Gunther said as he sat down. "I mean, we have the ability to do all this more or less out of the womb so educating control is important. What if you had gotten really angry at someone and slammed them with a lightning bolt accidentally?"

"That never happened. Maybe my parents did something to me so it wouldn't," I shrugged and took a bite. "I don't know. I never asked."

"Why not?"

"Before I was a ringmaster, I didn't really know to ask, I guess. Even visiting the Magical Midway as a kid, there weren't any other witches around besides my uncle, and I just assumed all of his crazy supernatural powers came from the circus. It just never dawned on me I could do any of it without his powers."

"Did you have a boyfriend?"

The question was so out of left field that my eyes shot up to stare at my friend in surprise. In the months that Gunther and I had known each other, we rarely talked about my old human life. Certainly not *that* part of my human life.

Okay, to be fair, that was never a part of my human life, so there wasn't much to talk about.

"It's hard to have an intimate relationship with someone when you can read people the way I can read people, and it's even harder when you can read them and can't tell them. I did have a fake boyfriend for a while," I told Gunther, and he choked on his pickle.

"A *fake* boyfriend? What's a fake boyfriend?"

"Aidan Parker. My friend, Tabitha, fixed me up with him. The first night we went on a date, I knew he was gay," I told Gunther, watching him closely. "His best friend Bobby is…was my friend Tabitha's fiancé. We were both kind of notorious for not dating. Obviously, we each had our reasons."

"What was his reason?"

"No one knew he was gay. He hadn't come out yet, and he was concerned that Bobby would reject him because of it. So he pretended to be straight."

"You two had something in common, then."

"I'm not gay!" I told him, shocked. "Not that there's anything wrong with that."

"No, I mean you both had something you were hiding from the world about yourselves."

"Oh. Right. Yeah, I guess. Only he admitted his secret to me."

"But you never told him yours."

I shook my head no. "I may not have known much about being a witch, but I always knew about *that* rule. In any case, we realized that Tabitha was fixing us up because she wanted us to do the double date thing, and so we would have dates to her wedding. We also realized that by pretending to be involved, we could enjoy a social life with our best friends. And we'd get them off our backs. No more blind dates."

"How'd that work out?"

"Great, for a while," I told him, pausing to take a bite out of my sandwich. After I swallowed, I continued. "But then Bobby found out Aiden was gay. He exploded and went ranting and raving to Tabitha. She came over to comfort me because in her mind, my heart was about to be broken and she felt guilty for fixing us up..."

"You told her the truth, didn't you?"

"I did and admitted I'd known from the first night he and I met. She was *furious* with me. She felt I violated her trust, like everything in our friendship for six months had been a lie."

I winced as I remembered Tabitha's face. The anger and hurt that twisted her features were physically painful to recall. When I came up with the plan with Aiden, I thought it would make her happy, even if it wasn't *precisely* accurate. And I told her the truth so she wouldn't feel guilty."

"She couldn't forgive you?"

By the time everything was said and done, our little foursome exploded. Tabitha and Bobby called off their wedding because Tabitha was shocked at how judgmental her intended husband was. Bobby and Aiden stopped being friends because Bobby was the homophobic jerk Aiden had been worried he was. Tabitha and I stopped speaking because Tabitha was furious that I had lied to her for so long. And Aiden, who felt responsible for the pain everyone was going through, withdrew.

"Yep. It happened a little over a month before I became ringmaster. So, *maybe* she would have forgiven me, eventually," I told him after taking a big gulp of iced tea. "I wasn't around anymore, though, to try and patch things up."

"Didn't you have any other friends that could have talked to her for you?"

"I didn't have any other friends *at all*," I told him as I got up to clear the plates. "Tabitha was a lucky find in college. People are remarkably honest about who they are in the privacy of their own minds, and they're almost *never* exactly who they present themselves to be. She *was,* though. She was guileless. I guess that's why she was so angry, though. She just couldn't understand what I had done because she never would have done it."

"You cared about her a great deal."

"I did," I told him as I washed the dishes. "I *do.* I don't know what I was thinking, not telling her. I'll always regret hurting her. She didn't deserve it."

"I'm sorry that you lost your friend, Charlotte."

"Two friends," I snapped. "Aiden was a lucky find, too. We may have faked a romantic relationship, but he and I were just as close as Tabitha and I were. And it was me that suggested the plan that blew our lives apart."

Tears ran down my face as I scrubbed the plates in my sink so hard that I thought the golden engravings would come off. I hadn't thought about Tabitha and Aiden in months, and the memories of them came rushing back over me in a waterfall of fond memories wrapped in pain. I sniffled.

"Charlotte," Gunther asked softly. "Are you all right?"

I cleared my throat. "I'm fine. Just give me a minute."

My head felt suddenly thick, and my eyes grew blurry. I shook my head to clear it, but the sparkling fog remained fixed before my eyes. "I'm not crying," I mumbled, dropping the plates and wiping my face with the soapy water. Now my eyes stung, and the fog continued to thicken.

"Need...towel...face funny..."

It was at that point everything went black.

CHAPTER 6

"DID YOU WANT ELVEN TEA?" BOLT ASKED AS I blinked up at him. My head felt as though it was wrapped in layers of wet gauze, and my body felt heavy.

"I…what? Where am I?"

"You're with me, of course," Bolt smiled. "Don't you remember?"

I remembered nothing.

The last thing that was clear in my mind was washing dishes in my yurt after Gunther and I ate lunch. He asked me about my life before the Magical Midway, and I told him about the awful situation with Aiden and Tabitha. Then my head got fuzzy…

"You glamorrred me," I slurred.

"I did no such thing, Charlotte," Bolt said as he handed me a china cup of tea. "You simply wanted to speak to me about the investigation that was going on. I think you may have drunk a bit too much of your human wine with that Makepeace at lunch. You must have fallen asleep when we came in here. Falling asleep, of course, is a polite term for passing out."

What Bolt said was impossible.

One protection the Magical Midway placed upon me was that alcohol of any kind did not affect me. Unfortunately, that same protection did not extend to poison. Wait a minute—how could that work for booze but not be possible for poison?

I should probably worry about that later.

I played along. I knew what Bolt was saying was impossible, but apparently *he* didn't know that. I remembered enough from college drinking to fake drunk as my mind cleared.

"Where's here?"

"We're in the Sticky Walls ride, of course. It's in elven mode, so we should be quite safe from the outside world while we talk," he said cordially as he sat down. "Though you may wish to sober up before we do so. Clearly, you are still inebriated."

Another wave of dizziness hit me, and I grabbed onto the rail to steady myself. Which was odd since I was sitting down.

Samson? Samson!

My guardian familiar cat didn't answer.

Uncle Phil?

Silence.

Since I was on the Magical Midway grounds, I knew that my powers were accessible. My defenses, too. The dizziness and vertigo made me loathe to try any magic, though, and I knew I needed help. The fear I had killed Chase with a misplaced tree was too fresh in my mind.

The silence that greeted my mind's voice, though, chilled me. I had grown used to having ready access to my uncle and that cat, and their absence made me feel very isolated and alone.

I needed to buy time for my head to clear or one of them to reappear in my mind.

"How long…have I…been here with you?"

"Here? Only an hour or so. The other hours we spent cavorting around the Magical Midway and the Werebear Jamboree were quite illuminating, Charlotte," Bolt said. "I had no idea you had such feelings for me. Though I must admit, I'm flattered that one such as yourself would be so attracted to me, being a lowly elven carnie and all."

That sobered me up rather quickly. I stared at the elf with suspicion.

Every spider-sense I had was screaming at me to be on alert. Bolt was calm, and I didn't sense he meant me any immediate harm, but he was hiding something. In fact, it felt like he was hiding a lot of somethings.

"What the heck are you talking about?"

"Are you sure you don't remember? I don't recall *everything* you said in your yurt, but I'm quite sure that Gunther will be able to recount it nearly word for word the next time you see him if you are curious," he told me as he leaned back casually against the image of a sparkling rock. "Your *friend* seemed quite jealous of your choice to spend time with me instead of him. You were quite…emphatic in your rejection of him."

I rubbed my eyes, desperately trying to push away the black curtain that had draped itself across my most immediate memories. It was as if someone had punched a hole in my life's timeline. I couldn't even access vague or hazy memories at all even though my mind was clearing.

Bolt smiled at me again and handed me a bubbly stemmed glass.

"I don't drink things offered by others," I told him as I pushed him away. "Especially not things offered to me by people I don't trust, and at the moment, Bolt, nothing coming out of your mouth makes any sense."

"I imagine most of the fairground feels the same way about your own drunken rant, Charlotte," Bolt said as he pulled back the glass and smiled. A ring of pure white metal with a sparkling blue stone flashed in the cold moonlight that streamed over us from the elven scenery. It was so bright for a moment that stars danced before my eyes. "You expressed a deep— and loud—aggravation with the former werebear leader. It was quite shocking, really."

"That's impossible. I didn't even know the man."

"Really? I never would have guessed from what you said."

Charlotte? Where are you?"

Samson, where the heck have you been?

Your uncle and I have been combing the Jamboree looking for you! Every paranormal in the place is talking about your behavior earlier today! What the heck got into you?

I don't know. I think…I think something was done to me. I'm in Sticky Walls, with Bolt.

We're coming.

"How did *you* know Chase Trout, Bolt?"

"I didn't. Never met the bear. Why do you ask?"

"How about Scout? He seemed awfully relieved to see you walk into that clearing the other night."

Bolt frowned, and a whirlwind of dizziness knocked into me aggressively like a crashing wave. My head fell against the wall as I gasped for air.

"Something wrong, Charlotte?" Bolt asked. "You really do need to learn to hold your wine a bit better. That might get you into trouble someday."

The blue and white room spun as vertigo ravaged me, and it was all I could do to hang on without sliding in a heap to the ground. As the blackness pulled me down again, I heard the door to the Sticky Walls open.

My last thought before I lost consciousness was that I'd never been so relieved to hear my uncle's voice before in my entire life.

～

The sound of people arguing greeted me when I clawed my way out of the blackness for the second time that day. At least, I think it was the same day. It could have been longer, and if I opened my eyes and talked to the angry people yelling at each other in my bedroom I could probably find out.

The chaotic debates, though, convinced me to keep my eyes closed just a bit longer.

"No one can *make* her say anything, Phil," Gunther snapped at my uncle. "Elves can glamour someone into saying how they really feel, but they can't influence them to say what they don't believe."

"I don't think you're correct, Gunther," Fortuna said quietly from a distant corner of the room away from me. "Nothing you are claiming Charlotte said to you are things I have ever read from her or felt from her. Not at all."

"Yeah, well, you haven't been doing this for long, have you? You've been a witch for, what, all of a month?"

I had never heard Gunther so angry before, and I certainly never heard him talk to Fortuna like that.

Stay asleep for now, Samson broke into my thoughts.

No one could sleep through this.

I mean you should keep your eyes closed. Let your uncle and Fortuna try to calm Gunther down. Your entrance into this discussion at this very moment is likely not going to help.

What the heck happened to me?

I'm embarrassed to say I don't know.

*You don't know? You don't **know**? Aren't you the one always telling me you know everything?* The steady presence of the cat's energy within my mind recoiled from my anger.

I was not on the Magical Midway grounds, Charlotte. There's a reason I don't go, and I don't leave. I have no strong connection to you or to this place when I am not physically on it while the power resides in you. If one of us is not here, our communication link is broken at the border.

Where were you?

I was...busy.

You were gorging yourself on salmon at the Werebear Jamboree, weren't you? I'm lying on this bed with a pounding headache because you were treating the festival like a cat all-you-can-eat buffet.

I said I was sorry. And I was looking for you while...snacking.

*You did **not** say you were sorry.*

Well. Perhaps. But I just did.

"I can't believe that you would accuse Charlotte of murder! You! The half-human witch that she saved just a month ago from a lifetime of being ostracized by his own people! From death! You, who helped to run the circus that kidnapped Mark! You, of all people! You don't trust *her* now?" Fiona shouted. I could hear Ningul's whispering as he tried to calm his girlfriend.

"I didn't say that. Don't put words in my mouth, and don't blame me for what people in my circus did to her. I never said I thought she killed anyone."

"No, you just said you don't know what to think about her drunken proclamations! The ones that she made about Chase Trout, who she never met, and you, who she now claims to despise, and Bolt, who she now claims to love."

I said what now?

From what I understand, Bolt entered your yurt as you and Gunther were finishing up lunch. You turned on Gunther and attacked him verbally, telling him you never wanted to see him again. You threw yourself into Bolt's arms, telling him you adored him. Then you and Bolt linked arms and went on a stroll through the Werebear Jamboree as you drunkenly proclaimed your glee over the death of Chase Trout to anyone that would listen.

Even my mind fell silent in shock as I absorbed Samson's words.

Charlotte, Uncle Phil broke into the cold emptiness of my head, *Gunther is simply hurt. His jealousy over Bolt is causing him not to think straight. Just give me a few moments more.*

I rolled over as unobtrusively as I could and pulled a pillow over my head. I didn't want to get up and deal with this, so if Uncle Phil thought he could fix it, he could have at it.

Laying in that bed, I felt ready to quit. No matter what I tried to do, everything at the Magical Midway and in the paranormal world felt like two steps forward and three steps back.

Charlotte, you are the most powerful witch in the world. On the planet. Maybe in the universe. That comes with benefits, but it also comes with a target. We have all had to deal with it to greater and lesser extents, Uncle Phil told me.

A big target, apparently, because people seem to have no problem hitting it.

"Son, I understand this is difficult for you. I see how you feel about my niece. I've seen it since the moment you laid eyes on her," Uncle Phil's soothing voice said from far away. "But have you stopped to think even once that separating her from you was the goal?"

"Well, clearly it was *her* goal. She went off with Bolt."

"Not *her* goal, Gunther," my uncle said gently. "*Someone's* goal. My niece may be the most powerful witch in the paranormal world, but *you* are the only other lawgiver. Isolating the two of you from one another is a perfect way to divide a power that intimidates many people. It would *certainly* make it easier to frame my niece for a murder that she didn't commit."

"And stoking *your* jealousy is a good way to make *you* act like a right git, Makepeace," Fiona growled. "Which you *are*. Acting like a right git, I mean. Ya kin'?

"Having Charlotte parade around in public telling everyone she's never met how much she disliked Chase Trout makes it much more likely no one will even suspect anyone else," Fortuna pointed out. "Honestly, Gunther, everything about this situation seemed designed to isolate Charlotte, and make her the clear suspect."

"But *how* could someone make her do that? How could someone make her say things that she didn't believe? That weren't true?" Gunther asked them. "She was *in* the Magical Midway."

"We program our defenses to fight against things we, or our ancestors, have faced, Gunther.

We have omnipotent power as ringmasters, yes. But we also have a responsibility to wield it, to shape it, to craft it. We are the minds behind the power," Uncle Phil explained. "If no one has fallen to an attack, would we know it could happen to defend against it?"

Maybe you should wake up now, Samson said.

Do I have to?

No. You could nap in bed until they come to take you away. That is one option. As a cat, I can't honestly fault you for considering that. The bed is quite comfy, and napping is quite relaxing. I'm sure you could nap quite frequently in jail.

~

I groaned loudly to announce my consciousness to the gathered throng in my yurt.

When I designed this living space, I *loved* the open-air one room arrangement. Everything was close to everything else, and like a true yurt, it was one big room. The drawback, though, was that my bedroom was just twenty feet away from the sitting area and the dining table.

I resolved to devise a new design that gave me a bedroom.

A private bedroom.

With a door.

Just make sure you install a cat door, Samson told me. I ignored him as I rolled over and looked at the crowd.

As my eyes met Gunther's, I felt the wave of pain and hurt that rolled through him like a storm. His eyes were clouded and dark, his body tense. He stood the farthest from my bed. From me.

"Gunther, I'm so sorry," I whispered, my voice hoarse.

"For what?"

"Honestly? I don't even know," I told him as I sat up. Fiona ran over to my bed and piled pillows behind my back to support me. As she pulled away, her hand extended with a glass of something that I took without question. As I sipped, energy flooded through my body, and I smiled a thank you.

"What do you mean, you don't *know?*" The edge in Gunther's voice stung me, but I put it aside for now.

"I mean I don't remember anything. I don't even know what day it is."

"We arrived yesterday."

"Good. Good. That means we haven't lost much time," I told him. "I don't think, anyway.

What time is it?"

"It's nearly sundown, Charlotte," Uncle Phil told me.

"So, I've had a blackout that lasted nearly the entire afternoon." I shuddered. "Obviously, considering the look on your faces, I wasn't curled up here in bed the entire time."

"No, you weren't," Fortuna told me.

"How long has it been since you got me from Bolt? How long have I been here?"

"An hour, perhaps. No more than that." Uncle Phil nodded.

"Thank you for that, by the way. I don't know what his plan was, but he seemed intent on keeping me there for a while."

"I think that elf has some things to answer for," Fiona fumed.

"You're probably right, but I don't know that confrontation is the best way to go, here," I told her, sipping more of the drink she brought me. "He's hiding something. No, that's not completely true. I mean, he is, but…"

"But what?" Gunther asked with gritted teeth.

"He's hiding *someone*," I told them, ignoring Gunther's bitterness. "When I woke up at his place, I could feel that there were things he was working to hide from me. Like he had stuffed facts and connections and thoughts into a big bag and sealed it away from me so I couldn't read them. It was *odd*. It was like nothing I had ever sensed before from anyone."

"Elves are secretive about their powers. While we know some things, we don't know *everything* that they can do. It is possible he has the ability to do something like what you just described. Highly possible, in fact," Uncle Phil said. "They are not inconsequential creatures."

I think that's a safe assumption, Samson agreed.

"Could he make me say the things I supposedly said with his glamour?"

"It's possible."

"Of course it is! You would never say that!"

"No."

"Maybe."

Fortuna, Fiona, Gunther, and Uncle Phil answered my question simultaneously. I ignored the pained answer from Gunther for the moment, hurt that he dismissed any possibility I was influenced. Jealousy, rejection, and anguish continued to swim within him, coloring everything he was saying.

"I'm going to take the three out of four," I smiled weakly. "Let's assume for the moment that he could make me say and do and act the way he wanted me to, and my protections are not as all-encompassing as we assume. Figuring out that he can and how he did it isn't nearly as important as figuring out why. Why would Bolt betray me like that?"

I thought back to everything Bolt said in the clearing to Wayland and Scout, and no matter how many times I went over it, I just couldn't understand what he was doing there or why he had gotten involved.

"Charlotte, wait, go back," Fortuna burst out.

"What?"

"The thing you're going over in your mind. Go back a bit. Go back to what Scout said about Bolt and the Elven code.

"Not when one is suspected of the murder, and the other has a history of protecting the one suspected," Bolt disagreed. *"Forgive my insinuation, Ringmaster, but we must ensure that the inquiry is above reproach."*

"You're a member of the Magical Midway. How is your assistance supposed to be above reproach?" Wayland asked.

"Elves are well known to cleave to the law," Scout told Wayland. *"His loyalty is to the highest law in the land based on the elven code. He's fine. Better than you."*

"Anything's better than those two witches!"
someone shouted from the crowd.

"That's it! Charlotte, *you* are *not* the highest law in the land." Fortuna said.

"The Witches' Council is," I said, and sighed.

"Oh, unicorns horns, are you *kidding me?* Those women again?" Fiona raged. Ningul, quiet as ever, folded her in his arms and hushed her. As usual, she accepted the affection while ignoring the suggestion she be silent. "I am getting right tired of those ninnies turning up in the middle of every single stinking problem that we have."

"It's just a theory. We don't know that they're the cause of this, or behind it, or orchestrating it. Whatever. It's just a theory," I told her.

"Want to take a bet on that?"

I looked at Fiona and shook my head no.

"Ya, didn't think so," she said smugly.

As we finished up verbalizing Fiona's suspicions about the Witches' Council, I sent everyone away one by one.

Except for Gunther.

My friend had been incredibly quiet during

our discussion, and when he did speak it was clear that he and I still had a problem.

"What?" he asked me sharply from across the room. I slipped out of bed and went over to him, seating myself far enough away that I didn't crowd him, but close enough to remove some of the distance between us.

"I don't know what I said to you today," I began quietly, leaning forward and staring at his face even though Gunther refused to look me in the eye. "It sounded like I was pretty terrible."

"No, just honest, I'm sure," he snapped, staring at his hands on his lap.

"Gunther, come on," I chided him. "Do I really strike you as the type of woman that would throw herself at some elf I barely know? The type of person that would say the things you implied I said?"

"I didn't *imply* anything. You said straight out that he was twenty times the man that I was, and that you would *never* be caught with someone like me if you didn't have to be," Gunther answered. "You *tore apart* my feelings for you in front of him. And then you *left* with him."

"What feelings for me? What are you talking about?"

Gunther sighed and flexed his fingers in his lap.

"Gunther, I don't know what you mean. Talk to me!"

"I talk to you *all the time*, Charlotte," Gunther said, finally looking up. "I flirt, and I imply, and I'm always here when you need me. I know that this transition has been hard for you, and I've tried to give you the space that you need to become the ringmaster that you need to be."

"And I appreciate that, Gunther."

"But I'm in love with you, and you treat it like it's nothing."

It felt like a bomb exploded in the middle of my living room. Despite what I just said to him, I knew that Gunther had some feelings for me. I didn't expect him to say what he said.

We stared at one another in silence.

I didn't know how to react to his declaration. I don't know that I believed it when he said it. I really thought that Gunther was only interested in me because he just hadn't been around anyone of his own kind that would give him the time of day as a half-witch.

As I looked at him, the pain and emotion playing in ripples across his face, the deep feeling rolling off him in waves toward me, I wondered how I could have dismissed my friend. How I could have missed it.

"Gunther—"

"Wait. Let me talk. You owe me that much."

I nodded and waited.

"Today, you did more than that. For the first time ever, you took my feelings seriously, and yet in that same moment, you threw them all back in my face. It hurt," he said. Gunther winced as I felt an explosion of pain shoot across the air at me. "I thought I was prepared to just be friends, to have you treat how I feel for you as some joke—"

"Gunther, I don't think it's a—"

"It *is* a joke to you. I know it is, but you've been my friend, and so I dealt with it. I hoped in time as you adjusted to this new reality that you would become more comfortable with who you are. I told myself that once you were, you'd see me differently. You'd start using your talent for seeing possibilities with us instead of with…well, everything else."

I winced under the projected onslaught. Waves of hurt, anger, confusion, and his broken heart washed over me. Whatever Gunther had been hiding from my intuition he now unleashed all over me, so there would be no misinterpreting his words. It was like a dam had burst.

I didn't know how I had gotten how he felt for me so wrong. I *was* wrong, though. I could feel it. He was utterly in love with me, and he wasn't working to hide it anymore. It was pouring over me, and it was so intense my eyes teared up.

"Gunther, I ignored your feelings because I knew that as soon as you walked into Impy, a thousand witches smarter and more beautiful than me would line up to go out with you," I told him. "I didn't want to get in the way of you finding the perfect woman."

"I already have," he said quietly.

"Oh, man, dude, I am so far from perfect. What did Wayland call me? A heat merchant?"

The corner of Gunther's mouth turned up in a slight smile.

"You really didn't mean what you said about Bolt?"

"I wish I could remember what I said to you, Gunther, but I don't. I don't have any idea what words I said to you. I can guess, though, if those words made you doubt me."

"I didn't, really," he said, leaning forward. "I was just hurt. I was angry."

"I get it. It's okay. How about I forgive you if you forgive me?"

"Done." Gunther reached out his hand

between us, and I leaned forward to pump it once.

"Again, I'm really sorry if what I said hurt you."

"I'll live," he told me, smiling widely. I felt all the love and pain recede back into him. It was like dust being sucked back into a vacuum cleaner, and I could feel him stuffing down the chaos of emotions once again.

"I wish you *wouldn't* do that," I told him.

"Do what?"

"Shove everything you feel down like that," I told him. Getting up from the chair, I stood up and moved to sit next to him. The air tingled with energy as I closed the distance between us. I grabbed his hand and held it firmly. "I've never felt as close to anyone in my life as I do to you, Gunther. Surely you know that."

Gunther squeezed my hand but remained silent. His breathing had become shallow, and I could feel a fog of hopefulness surrounding him.

"I...I haven't really let myself feel anything more than friendship for you. I guess I stuff, too," I smiled. "I knew that we both had our circuses and our family obligations, and I just never really entertained the idea that we *could* find a way around them to have anything more than a friendship."

"I think we can," he said. "I think you and I can do anything, Charlotte. After all, one day we'll be the two most powerful witches in the entire world. Surely, *one* of the benefits of that has to be that we can find a way to make a relationship work."

I snickered despite myself, and Gunther laughed.

As our laughter faded, I looked into Gunther's eyes and wondered how I could've *ever* thought I would be able to avoid falling hard for this man.

Maybe it wouldn't work out.

Maybe I would get my heart broken when he became ringmaster, and we could never be together.

Maybe I would be alone, pining for him once this was all over.

But feeling how much he cared about me, and knowing how much I cared about him, I realized this was unavoidable from the beginning.

I had to try.

Even if it broke my heart someday.

"I do care about you, Gunther. A lot. I'm sorry if my avoidance of the issue has come off like indifference or rejection. I didn't mean for it to. I just didn't see a way this could work. But I'm willing to try."

I could detect a surge of disappointment I didn't say those three little words back after his opening declaration, but Gunther stuffed it down quickly. I refused to feel guilty, and I was grateful that he accepted what I had to give for now.

I just couldn't go there yet. I had barely allowed myself to think about us romantically before.

I needed time.

"It can, Charlotte. I know it can. I really want to try, too."

"I've never really done this before," I told him, blushing.

"Done what?"

"Any of this. Boys, a boyfriend...I've had a lot of first dates. But that's it." Gunther put his arm around me, resting my head on his shoulder. He felt warm and safe...And oh, man, he smelled good.

"That's okay, Charlotte, I've never done it, either. We'll figure it out together. Deal?"

"Deal, Mr. Makepeace," I told him, sighing.

CHAPTER 7

"YOU ARE TWO DAYS AWAY FROM BEING BROUGHT up on charges, and you decided to get a boyfriend *now*?" Anya asked me after I informed her of the conversation between Gunther and me. She had been claiming almost since the beginning that we would get together someday. It seemed only fair to let her know she was right.

May as well get the smug satisfaction over with.

"Maybe Charlotte just wants to ensure he can visit her in prison," Faleena told her. The werebear female had reacted strangely to my announcement, but when I poked further into her reaction empathically, her thoughts and emotions folded up like a flower. "Though I can't believe she chose that boring Makepeace boy over that sexy elf she was running around with yesterday."

My eyes narrowed. Wasn't it just yesterday that Faleena was talking down about elves in general, and Bolt specifically? Now he's the sexy elf?

"I don't know what happened yesterday," I told Faleena. "I think it was just too much wine affecting me."

Anya looked at me strangely. I stared at the naiad hoping that she wouldn't divulge my secret immunity to drunkenness, a secret I did not want more widely known for the moment. Her eyes flashed to Faleena, and then back to me. The naiad's expression looked troubled for a moment and then smoothed out as she laughed.

"Witches are pairing up all over the place, it seems," Gunther said as he walked upon us. He immediately draped his arm lightly around me and leaned down to give me a light kiss on the cheek. I blushed. "Scout has a new relationship as well."

"With a witch?" I asked, surprised.

"From Impy," he said. "The rumor is she's quite close to the Witches' Council."

"Why would that have anything to do with

anything?" Faleena asked sharply. "Are there witches *not* close to the Witches' Council? Besides you all and your little migrant rebellion, I mean."

I was beginning to genuinely dislike Anya's friend, but despite my extensive witch and lawgiver and ringmaster powers, I couldn't quite figure out what it was about the werebear that bothered me.

"I think some are closer than others," I responded.

"Charlotte, we should go and say hello. We are all witches, after all, and it's the proper etiquette in a situation like this, since you and I are considered leaders," he said. "If you'll excuse us, ladies, even in the midst of controversy we must stand on polite protocol."

We said our goodbyes and made our way toward the Jamboree, leaving Faleena looking annoyed as we walked away.

"Is it my imagination, or was Anya's friend a little too defensive about Scout's new witch girlfriend?" Gunther asked me as we walked toward the front of the Magical Midway.

"Are you developing intuition, Gunther?" I asked him.

"Everyone has intuition, Charlotte. Yours may

be profoundly powerful, but I've got *a little*, you know."

"Not enough to know I wasn't really into Bolt," I told him sweetly and felt Gunther's arm tense around me.

"You're not going to let me forget that for a while, are you?"

"Nope. Girlfriend prerogative."

"I like that," he said and gave me a squeeze.

"What?"

"That you just called yourself my girlfriend."

"You're going to be one of *those* boyfriends, are you?"

"Ooh, I think I like that, too," he told me as he laughed.

"You're right, though. There's something about Faleena that just doesn't seem...I don't know. Right? Normal? I can't figure it out, honestly. But I'm having a tough time liking the woman."

As we stepped across the boundary that separated the Magical Midway from the Werebear Jamboree festival grounds, Bolt emerged from the trees and walked straight for us.

"There is *no way* this is happening again," Gunther mumbled angrily. He dropped his arm from around my shoulder and rapidly moved his hands. As he clapped them together, I felt a shimmering curtain descend around us. It was pink, and it smelled like roses. "That should fix him."

"What did you do?"

"A love protection spell," he said as we moved closer to the elf. "If he's using his seduction glamour on you to cause these blackouts and dizzy spells, this should prevent that. For the next couple of days, you won't be able to be attracted to anyone other than me."

"That's…kind of…coercive, Gunther," I told him, my independent female bubbling up indignation within me. "You could've *asked*, you know. Actually, you *should* have asked."

"It's just a shield, you can break it if you want to. It was the fastest thing I could come up with that I thought would work," he said. "Besides, it doesn't really affect you unless you want it to. It's not like people don't see it coming when you cast it. The rose smell is almost overpowering."

While that was true, I still wasn't sure I was okay with it.

I was sure I wasn't okay with what Bolt was doing to me, though, so I didn't remove it. If I stopped to examine my feelings about it, I reluctantly admitted that having a boyfriend throw a shield around me in an instant seemed kind of cute.

Especially at the rate I kept becoming a target.

It's estimated that one hundred and eight billion people have lived on the planet. As I watched Bolt walk up to us, seven and a half billion people were alive on the planet, give or take. That's 6.9% of those who have ever lived.

Once, paranormals had been 1% of the population.

Now, according to the census the Witches' Council took every three years, we were just.0005%.

Only thirty-seven and a half thousand paranormals, give or take.

On the whole planet.

And yet I kept meeting ones that wanted to do me in. I wondered what the statistics were surrounding *that*?

"Well, it seems I've been displaced by the very one you rejected yesterday, Charlotte," Bolt said as he met us on the path. "You are very fickle with your men, Ringmaster. Paired up with one, one day, and on to another the next."

The tea rose fog shimmered and energy buzzed around Gunther and me.

Your boyfriend's shield is repelling the elf's magic, Samson said.

Decided to come with us, did you?

I am quite ashamed that I could not help you yesterday. I do not like feeling ashamed. That's not a familiar feeling, you know. Whichever side of the boundary you choose to be on, I will be on that one as well.

What about the Magical Midway? Doesn't that leave them in danger?

We are too close to the Werebear Jamboree for a specific attack from the Witches' Council. Too many people would see. The circus will be fine without us for a few hours. Just remember the sunrise and sunset rule. We must return before the sun dips below the horizon.

"What do you need, Bolt?" Gunther asked the elf.

"Scout would like a word with you both," he responded pleasantly. "He asked me to accompany you."

"What a coincidence!" I said. "We were just on our way to his camp. We have been told a witch from Impy is attending the Werebear Jamboree, and we thought we would pay our respects."

"Of course you did," Bolt smiled. "If you'll follow me then."

I don't like this, Samson said.

Me, neither, Uncle Phil broke in.

Is there anyone left at the Magical Midway guarding anything?

I've asked the ghosts to leave the haunted house and patrol the grounds, Samson said. *If they spot anything, they can teleport instantly and let me know. We'll be able to rubber band back to the Magical Midway with no delay.*

Gunther and I followed Bolt further into the forest. The path turned from the more populated camping areas into a much denser section of trees. The sunlight struggled to shine through the thick canopy, and the air grew chill and moist.

"Hurry along," Bolt called over his shoulder. "You wouldn't want to be late, now, would you?

"How can we be late if no one knew we were coming?"

Bolt didn't respond.

The path grew darker, and large werebears now lined either side. Each held a weapon while standing at attention, and their eyes followed us suspiciously.

Samson, I can bring Gunther back with me the same way I brought Mark back from the Makepeace Circus, correct? Just grab his hand and say the magic word?

Yes, why?

I just want to make sure. I don't know that we're in any danger, but the atmosphere out here is feeling a little ominous. If I must leave quickly, I don't want to leave him out here alone.

Aw, that's very cute, Samson said. Then he sent a retching noise into my mind.

Cut it out, cat, and let me concentrate.

Samson grew silent, but I could still feel his presence in my mind. After yesterday's isolation, it was good to feel the accompaniment of my familiar riding shotgun. Just as the forest grew so dark I questioned whether we could see our way forward, fires illuminated the path, and a cave appeared through the trees.

The werebear guards along either side of the path grew bigger the closer we got to the cave. Their weapons shone in the glow of the fires.

"Not the most cheerful place to hang your hat," I commented when we stepped into a clearing in front of the cave. The mouth of it was at least ten feet tall and twenty feet wide. The mountain that capped it was the outer ring boundary of the top of the mesa.

"I'd welcome you to my home," Scout said as he emerged from the darkness within the cave, "but this isn't really a friendly visit, is it? And it shouldn't even be my home anymore."

"Well, we *started* out on a friendly visit," I told him cheerfully. "We understand that you have a witch staying with you, and we wanted to come and pay our respects. If it's about to turn unfriendly, Scout, it's not because of us."

"Oh, I doubt you have any respect for me, ringmaster," a dark-haired woman stepped out from behind Scout. She was dressed head to toe in black, wearing a crown of woven branches. The ends of those branches were red as if they had been dipped in blood. "I am a huntress witch. Your kind has despised my kind for generations."

"I'm not sure if you've heard about me? But I'm new here. I don't even know what a huntress witch is, much less have any reason why I should despise you."

"They're witches that hunt and kill prey, Charlotte." Gunther squeezed my hand and pulled me closer to him. "They track and kill the weak for sport, for honor, and—"

"For a price when the motivation for the hunt

is honorable," the mysterious woman finished. "My ancestors have picked off the weak members of your circuses for generations now. Your protections are so strong and so great that victims from the magical fairs are the most prized of all the prey."

"Well, *that's* really dark and disturbing," I told her.

"The paranormal world is not all unicorns and cotton candy, ringmaster," the woman said. "I enjoy the dark corners where the unicorns fear to enter."

"*This* is your girlfriend?" I asked Scout.

"My *partner*, Devana, is much more than a *girlfriend*," Scout sneered. He wrapped a powerful arm around the menacing woman and jerked her toward him. I felt a wave of impatience explode out from her for just a second. A moment later, it was gone, covered by something that felt sort of like affection.

Sort of.

Scout's intense attraction and lust for the woman was clearly legitimate. Devana's feelings for him?

Maybe not so much.

"What did you ask us here for, Scout?" Gunther asked when Scout didn't expand on exactly why Devana was much more than a girlfriend. "We've done what we came to do. What do you want?"

"I want to know why your little girlfriend was running around my Werebear Jamboree telling everyone how much she hated my brother," he responded. "The elf here told me that it was clear to everyone that she despised him."

Devana glared at Bolt and then looked away.

For a moment, I thought about coming up with some kind of cover story, but at the last second, I decided to just be honest with him. I did not understand at this point who had killed Scout's brother. A conspiracy swirled around his murder, but I had no proof Scout knew.

You have no proof he didn't, so tread carefully, Samson told me.

"I don't know what you're talking about, Scout. I wish I did, because I'm a little confused myself," I told him. "I don't remember much of yesterday afternoon."

"The lady ringmaster had imbibed of some human wine, future clan leader," Bolt told Scout. He stepped away from us toward Devana. "I would not be surprised if she truly did not remember the terrible, disrespectful things that she said about your honored brother."

"The woman went off with you, did she not, as she spoke her anger?" Devana asked Bolt.

"I did spend the afternoon with her, yes."

"Odd. And yet she is clearly wrapped in the lawgiver's protection. A spell that only works for those in a committed relationship." Devana waved her hand and the pink haze that surrounded Gunther and me suddenly blazed brightly. "It seems that your little romantic interlude was not a genuine one, elf. One wonders if her words were genuine when she roamed with you, considering that."

"What is your problem, witch?" Bolt asked, angered.

"I am simply a huntress," she responded. She squatted down, grasping a handful of dirt. "I hunt those that are weak. I cull the herd when needed to keep the balance." She extended her hand as the dirt spilled out from within her palm and fell back to the earth. "I take down those that need to be taken down. For the good of all, of course."

Clapping the dirt from her hands, she shrugged.

"That is not an answer," Bolt told her.

"The balance is always my answer. The *weak* are my target. Those who cannot see the truth. Those who are too weak to survive. Those who challenge the order. And the weak are not always the ones that people assume they are. Are *you* weak, elf? How about *you*, ringmaster?"

"If you're really taking me on, lady, I think you're about to find out," I told her.

"That was not an answer," the woman responded. "When you answer that question, you will know why I am here."

"Who hired you?" Gunther asked Devana, pulling me closer.

"Who hired her for what?" Scout asked, confused. "What the heck are you witches talking about? I feel like I'm missing something."

"Don't worry about it, darling, you'll understand soon enough." Devana patted Scout's shoulder as if he were her pet. "Everyone here will get what they want or what they deserve. Sometimes, those things may even be the very same. Many times, they will not be."

Bolt's blue ring flashed as a beam of sunlight broke through the canopy, and he quickly shoved his hand into his pocket to hide it. The shield around us suddenly crackled loudly, then stopped just as immediately.

"Get us out of here, Charlotte," Gunther told me. The shield around us buzzed and then crackled again.

"I'm not done with you yet!" Scout shouted.

"Now, Charlotte," Gunther said more urgently, grabbing my hand tightly.

I flung us both back to the Magical Midway turning over in my mind what on earth I had just seen and working through what it all meant.

"That buzzing and crackling was an attack," Gunther told me as we reappeared in my yurt back in the Magical Midway. "I didn't want to wait around and see if it was stronger than my hastily thrown up shield."

"I thought you said it would repel any glamour from Bolt."

"It would. But the shield wouldn't react like that against a glamour."

"The attack was coming from someone else in that clearing. It had to be," Uncle Phil said as he walked in, Samson trotting behind him. "You two all right?"

"We're fine," I shrugged. "I didn't even realize anything was going on. I just got us out of there because Gunther said something."

"Charlotte, sometimes your statements really don't inspire confidence, dear girl."

I made a face at my uncle.

"What would a werebear leader be doing with a huntress witch?" I asked as we sat down.

"Do you know what a huntress witch is?"

"No. Well, nothing more than Gunther said back in the clearing. That was the first I've ever heard of them."

"Don't you think we should start there?"

I got it. My uncle had to make sure he pointed out that I didn't know enough to do my job, protect myself, or solve the case. Yep. Why should anyone miss a moment to remind me that I've only been doing this less than six months and I suck at it?

There are things that you must know about the huntress witch. Phil is not merely trying to make fun of your lack of knowledge. Although, point of fact, that wouldn't exactly be hard.

Really? Things I couldn't tell from her all-black outfit, the crown of bloodied branches, and her oracular pronouncements?

We know you realize she's dangerous, Charlotte. Your uncle just wants you to understand why she's dangerous.

"Okay, then enlighten me, gentlemen. Please, let's take some time to fill in the large gaps in my education. Gaps, I remind you, that are not my fault."

"At some point, Charlotte, enough time will have passed in your tenure as ringmaster that your father's decision not to educate you as a witch won't be an acceptable excuse anymore," Uncle Phil told me with the force of a hammer coming down. "Perhaps that's not today, but I do think it's coming very soon."

"Hey, Phil, lighten up a little bit on her, okay?" Gunther told my uncle, shifting uncomfortably in his seat. "I went to school for eight years to know what I know. She's had less than six months."

"She's had five months," Uncle Phil snapped at Gunther. "And that doesn't matter. She's facing threats that no ringmaster in our history has ever faced in such a short period of time. If you truly care about my niece, Gunther Makepeace, you will stay out of the relationship between us and stay quiet when I instruct the ringmaster of *our* circus on what she needs to know."

"Mr. Astley, I meant no offense—"

"You children never do, and yet you keep making decisions that blunder our entire community into highly volatile situations." Uncle Phil stood up for no other reason than to look down upon us both.

Where is this coming from, Samson?

You realize I can hear you when you talk to the cat, don't you? Uncle Phil said in my head as he stared down at me.

I don't care if you can hear me or not, the way you're talking to Gunther is entirely uncalled for.

Uncle Phil's eyes narrowed.

Do you realize the two of you just advertised that you are in a romantic relationship? In a clearing lined with guards, with a huntress witch that might be here to hunt you down, at one of the largest festivals in the paranormal world? And you did this all while there's talk of you being a murderer?

Gunther took a breath to speak, but I reached out and placed my hand on his arm to still him. He looked at me and then turned to look up at Uncle Phil. I was impressed that he intuited Uncle Phil and I were speaking because he squeezed my hand and stayed silent.

Well, when you put it like that...Actually, I don't get it. Why does Gunther and me dating have anything to do with any of this?

You are a ringmaster and a lawgiver. He is a lawgiver and a ringmaster heir. You think the Witches' Council feared you before? How about the two of you being in a relationship? What do you think they will think about that, Charlotte?

Honestly, Uncle Phil, I don't care one whit what the Witches' Council thinks about who I date.

Perhaps you should. Your boyfriend is not a ringmaster yet. The physical protections that keep you from so much harm do not extend to him. Should the Witches' Council decide that the two of you together is too much of a threat, Gunther is now a much easier target to destroy than you.

My stomach dropped to the dirty floor of my yurt and stayed there.

I don't have to be telepathic to know that you understand what I'm saying now, don't you?

I nodded silently, quietly kicking myself for thinking anything I did anymore wouldn't have far-reaching consequences. Of all the things that ran through my head when taking a chance with Gunther, his physical safety was not one of those considerations.

What about the lawgiver protections?

They will help some, yes. But there's a reason that ring can go so quickly from one person to another upon death. Their defenses are not in the same league as the ringmaster protection. And your enemies have been finding gaping holes in your own protections.

I didn't know who came up with rings being so crucial in the paranormal world, but it seemed ridiculous. Not that they weren't relevant in the human world. I mean, wedding rings were significant because of what they signified. Engagement rings.

The symbolic human value of rings is a shadow of the power of rings in our own, Samson said.

So many rings causing so many problems. The lawgiver ring, the Vanya ring…Wait a minute.

That *couldn't* be the ring on Bolt's finger.

It's impossible.

Wasn't it?

"We need to get everyone together," I told Gunther, who jumped as I unexpectedly broke the silence. "I think my *uneducated* mind may have just realized why Bolt is involved in this, and who's behind it all."

CHAPTER 8

"When Mark was kidnapped, Fiona and I went to talk to Bolt. He used to date Alexa Atwater, and since she showed up the same day that Mark disappeared we wanted to see what we could find out about her," I told the group.

"I'd never been in the Sticky Walls ride when it was in the elven mode before. Unbelievably beautiful," Fiona interjected as she grabbed a chip from the bowl on the table in front of her. "All blue and white and sparkling. Just so pretty."

"He told us the story of what happened when he and Alexa broke up."

"What does that have to do with anything now, Charlotte?" Fortuna asked.

"She left him because of greed. At least, that's

what it sounded like. She stole his Vanya ring. Well, I don't know if stole is the right word. He gave it to her as an engagement ring," I explained.

"*Vanda* ring. Vanya was the word he said to create it. And she sold it to a witch in Impy," Fiona said. "Broke his heart, too. And ruined his life, really, since elves only get one Vanya ring. Ugh, Vanda ring. Now you have me doing it, Charlotte."

I rolled my eyes.

"Okay, how about we just call it the elf one ring? Anyway, the one ring is a pledge ring, and it has magical properties that make it really valuable, he said," I told them.

"Does he have to bring it to Mordor?" Fortuna chuckled. I glared at her. "Sorry, I kinda had to. I mean, you really did walk into that one."

"I think I liked you better when you were shy," I told her as everyone else looked confused. "Anyway, she made some deal with the witch in Impy to use one of the safety nets of the ring. You speak the word Vanda after moving the ring to a different finger and all the wealth of the person you're engaged to transfers to you."

"Vanya," Fiona corrected. "It's a Vanda ring. The word is Vanya. That transfers all of the money from one person to another instantly."

"I'm familiar with that," Uncle Phil said. "That only works if the person who gifted the ring is dead, though. Bolt's not dead."

"Nope, he's not, but that didn't matter. Not when a witch in Impy City helps you steal the wealth of your fiancé magically, apparently. She found someone that knew how to get around the whole Bolt being dead thing. She stole his money, and kept the ring, I guess."

"I asked Alexa about the ring, actually, after we caught her," Fiona said. "I wanted to try and get it back for Bolt. It seemed horribly sad that he would wind up living alone the rest of his life. She told me there were other powers in the ring. Leaving it with the witch was the price of her help."

"Do we know who this witch was?" Fortuna asked Fiona.

"No, why?"

"I don't know. I was just curious, I guess."

"So, the whole point of me telling the story was that twice now a ring on Bolt's hand has caught my eye. The stone is the same blue color as the rocks in the Sticky Walls ride when it mimics whatever Elvish land it's trying to resemble," I concluded.

"That doesn't mean it's the one ring," Fiona said.

"Precioussss!" Fortuna whispered.

"Are you kidding me?"

"Sorry, Charlotte. Really. I'm really sorry," Fortuna mumbled. She pulled her legs up and wrapped her arms around them. "I don't know what's got into me, really. I'll stop."

"How do we find out if it's the one ring? Who would know what they look like?" I asked. Fiona's face tightened with concentration.

"Well, an elf, I guess. But he's the only one here."

"Maybe Samson knows," Uncle Phil suggested.

I do.

"He does, actually," I told the group. We all waited silently.

"So is it the ring?" Fiona asked.

"I don't know, he hasn't told me yet."

Everyone in the group turned to look at the cat lying on the bed. Samson was curled peacefully against my pillow, his tail wrapped around his coiled body. His breath was even and steady.

Are you going to tell us or not?

Tell you what?

If that ring on Bolt's finger is the same ring that Alexa sold to the witch in Impy?

You didn't ask me that.

Yes, I did.

No, you asked me if I knew the answer to that. And I told you I did.

There were so many word games I liked.

I liked Scrabble. I loved playing Hangman when I was a kid. Sunday crossword puzzles with Dad were fun. Mad libs at a party! That was fun. I *loved* word games. *All* sorts of word games.

But Samson word games?

I hated Samson word games.

Samson, my honored familiar, Guardian of the Magical Midway, sleeper on my pillow, eater of the salmon—could you pretty please, with sugar on top, tell me if the ring that Bolt is wearing is the same Vanya ring he gave to Alexa?

Vanda ring.

Samson!!

Yes. It is the same ring. What was once stolen from him has now been restored to him.

How?

That is the question, isn't it? When one works that hard to get a thing, one rarely gifts it back to the one stolen from for no reason, I would think.

I related the information I got from Samson

to the group. For a moment, Fiona smiled, and I felt relief flow from her that Bolt had his future restored to him. Despite his actions of the past few days, Fiona still cared for him.

As soon as she felt that relief, however, it dribbled away in a cauldron of confusion, and then concern.

"No witch from Impy would just hand that back to him for no reason," she said. "All his money, all his power, everything was just handed back to him?"

"According to Samson, yes."

"I wonder what the price is on something like that?" Gunther mused as he fidgeted with his lawgiver ring. "Is it worth it to sell out your ringmaster to get your future back?"

"They can be cold and calculating creatures, elves," Uncle Phil said.

"Dishonest and disloyal, too, clearly," Fiona said. "Bolt has been with us for years. I *never* would've thought this of him."

"Look, I'm not letting anyone off the hook for what they did. Whatever that ultimately winds up being," I told Fiona. "But if you had lost the hope of a marriage, of children, and also lost everything your ancestors and family had given to you because of one bad decision...if someone gave you the opportunity to take that back, what would you do? What would any of us do?"

"You're too understanding, Charlotte," Gunther said as Uncle Phil and Fiona nodded. "Even if he was approached and manipulated by some witch to do this, even if he *only* did it to get that ring back—look, there are just some lines you don't cross."

"He already *has* the ring, Charlotte," Fortuna pointed out. "I hate to agree with everyone else, but this isn't something being held over him. He wasn't told to do whatever he's doing, and *then* he would get the ring. It's not leverage."

"She's right. He has the ring. He's just as guilty as whoever is directing him." Fiona leaned into Ningul. He put his arm around her and rubbed her shoulder, but said nothing when she sighed.

Which I was getting used to from the centaur any time he was around Fiona. I would need to stop by a centaur meeting at some point just to re-familiarize myself with the man's voice.

It was late. Despite the hour being close to midnight, we hadn't come up with any formalized plan. I was nervous that we would figure out none of this in time. Tomorrow was the last full day we had left.

Knowing *why* Bolt was acting the way he was didn't get me any closer to understanding what was ultimately behind the werebear leader's murder, or the determination to pin it on me.

I wasn't even sure Chase's murder was connected with the effort to frame me. They could just be two unconnected conspiracies, each with their own perpetrators and reasons. Maybe someone killed him and then just saw an opportunity to get rid of me, too. Maybe—

"Charlotte, do you want me to go?" Gunther asked me as soon as the last of our friends and family left my yurt. I turned to look at my boyfriend…

…my boyfriend.

Just thinking of Gunther as my boyfriend seemed strange and unfamiliar. As soon as we were alone, nervous tension had replaced the ease I felt around him. The decision to attempt a relationship opened up so many possibilities.

Possibilities I wasn't ready for.

"I…um…I don't want you to go, but I don't want you to read too much into the fact that I don't want you to go. If you get my meaning," I told Gunther as I blushed so many shades of red that I imagined I must look like a tomato on the verge of exploding.

"The only thing that I'm reading into your desire not to have me leave is that you'd like me to be here with you. That's all," Gunther said as he stepped forward.

"Okay. That's good, then. I guess."

Way to go, Charlotte. That wasn't awkward.

You said it. I didn't.

Shut up, Samson.

"How come you didn't bring Delilah with you?" I asked Gunther as I stepped over to my stove and put on a kettle for tea. I found myself missing his kitten familiar. "Isn't she lonely without you?"

"She still very young, yet, and I didn't feel like a festival was a good place for her. She somewhat rambunctious, and doesn't think things through very well," he said as he moved the circled chairs back to the dining table. "She likes you, you know."

"I'm a very likable person," I told him, regaining some of the confidence I had before I stumbled.

"Hopefully, that will get around soon, and people will stop trying to kill you, kidnap you, or glamour you."

"Hey, no one's tried to kill me."

"Alexa and the water snake?"

"Oh." I had forgotten about Anya's naiad sister and the slow-moving, relentless poisoned water snake. That wasn't really a conspiracy to kill me, though. That was an attack of opportunity. "You're right. I forgot about the water snake."

I fell silent again, rinsing out the cups my friends had used. I didn't know what I was supposed to do with a boyfriend. When Aidan and I had faked a relationship, it was easy. We were just friends, and there was no pressure. It wasn't going anywhere.

Now...now there was pressure.

"You're so quiet all of a sudden, Charlotte," Gunther observed behind me. "Is everything okay?"

Sure. Everything's fine. You told me that you're in love with me, and I don't know what I'm supposed to do with that. I don't know if I'm in love with you. But, you know, let's just pretend none of that ever happened.

Are you talking to me or talking to yourself? Samson asked.

Get out of my head, Samson. Seriously.

"Charlotte?"

"I'm sorry," I told Gunther as I turned off the

water, finished with the busywork I was using to avoid him. Turning around, I leaned against the counter and crossed my arms. "I'm not sure how this works. I just...to be honest, all of a sudden I'm not sure what I'm supposed to say to you."

"Okay, that's a good place to start, I guess," Gunther said, gesturing to the couch with a smile. "Thank you for being honest with me, at least. To be honest with you in return, my biggest worry is that you would just push me away completely. Again."

"I don't do that."

"You kinda do," Gunther smiled as we sat down. "You're really good at compartmentalizing, Charlotte. I think it's what's allowed you to get good at this paranormal thing so quickly."

I burst out laughing. Gunther raised his eyebrow. "Wait a minute, you're serious?" I asked him as my laughter trailed off.

"Of course I'm serious. I think you've been thrown a bigger change than any paranormal I've ever known, with the possible exception of Mark and Fortuna," Gunther said seriously. "No matter what tries to knock you off your feet, you get right back up again. I don't think you realize how impressive it is."

"Stop. I'm serious, just stop," I told him.

"There isn't a moon cycle that's gone by yet where someone's life hasn't been threatened. Or lost."

"And last month, you saved three people. Me, Fortuna, and Mark. I'd add the lion pride to that, as well, when you came up with this citizen legal system."

"I didn't come up with that," I argued. "That was based on the human world that I came from." And a television show I watched a lot of. But I decided not to mention that.

"And Alessandra?"

"Okay, just stop. I get it, I've done some not so harmful things that made life marginally better for some people," I told him.

"You've done that, though, by juggling all of the competing needs people have from you. I've become one more need, and I get that can feel like pressure. Compared to catching a murderer or keeping you out of jail, working on a new relationship doesn't really seem like a wise way to spend your time."

"Geez, Gunther, are you arguing for or *against* our relationship here?"

"What I'm saying is I thank you for not simply pushing me out, or ignoring me to focus on the other things," he said. "I would be the easiest problem to ignore. And you're not doing that."

Gunther reached across the couch and gently took my hand.

"What I'm trying to say is I want to be a *help* to you, not just one more obligation you have to learn to juggle. Believe it or not, I have some understanding of what it's like to be in a relationship with a ringmaster," he pointed out. "I watched my mother and my father for a number of years before she passed away. I know the toll it can take on a partner. I go into this with eyes wide open, Charlotte."

"How did you get to be so kind and understanding?" I asked him, squeezing his hand.

"Childhood tragedy, and teenage isolation, I suppose," Gunther said seriously. "It's not a pathway to empathy that I would recommend. But it *was* mine."

"I'm sorry I'm such a weirdo," I told him, scooting closer to Gunther on the couch. I laid my head on his shoulder. He pulled me gently forward to wrap one arm around me so I could snuggle in. With my body in such close proximity to his, his thoughts and emotions became more evident the longer we touched.

Well, that was a side effect I wasn't aware of.

"You are *my* weirdo," he said, sighing. "Don't ever apologize for who you are, Charlotte. I couldn't imagine you any other way."

Gunther tucked me in and then settled in on the couch for the night. I felt safer with him in the yurt, but nervous that falling asleep would lose us time we couldn't afford to give away to rest.

"You're *already* asleep," Ethel Elkins snapped. "Get with the program, eh? We need to talk, so get up. Time moves strangely in dreams so we may not have much of it."

I struggled to open my eyes, sure that I had not fallen asleep yet. When I opened them (or I thought I'd opened them), I was in a sunlit meadow I didn't recognize. Twenty feet away from me, the gnarled old woman leaned against a tree at the center of the clearing. Like her, the tree was enormous, her bejeweled cane leaning against it.

"What is this place?"

"It's a *meadow*," she squawked as her hand slammed down against the thick trunk. "You're dreaming, I pull you out of the dream, I talk to you, and with all those things happening your

first question is *where we are*? You're in a meadow!
In a dream! If you keep questioning the obvious,
girly, things are going to take you much longer
than they should!"

Why did everyone from the Makepeace
Circus feel the need to call me girly?

I thought I was still lying in bed, but I was
standing with my feet firmly on the ground.
Everything seemed so real. I could smell the
heady scent of the spring flowers, feel the warm
breeze over my skin. I looked down at a simple
white cotton shift that draped me. My feet were
bare upon the softest grass.

"Why am I here?"

"Because you're dreaming!" Ethel said with
exasperation. The old woman rolled her eyes and
looked up at the leaves of the enormous tree that
shaded her. "This is really who you picked?
Really? You couldn't give me something easier to
work with?"

Ethel Elkins was a norn. She lived at the
Makepeace Circus and waddled around like a
crazy old woman. At least the norn had every
time I had seen her, which wasn't frequently, but
the old woman made one heck of an impression.
Gunther seemed to have a particular affection for
her, and she for him. I sensed it from them both.

She was confusing, though.

She would rant and cackle about prophecies and the future, destinies, and balls and I don't know what else. I didn't know what to make of her rantings then, and I wasn't sure what to make of her showing up in my dreams now.

Except for one thing.

My dreams have always been the *one* place I can't sense anyone else, even if I try. Not my uncle, not Samson, and not any mental image of anyone else that may show up for a joint jaunt through my subconscious. It's been the one time of day where I can be alone with my own thoughts.

I was sensing thoughts and feelings from the old woman.

What's more, there was a…a *presence* here, and I was sensing thoughts and feelings from it, too.

Not just here. Everywhere, really. It had thoughts and emotions and feelings and they were all around me. They were so vast, so overpowering that it chilled me to the bone.

"*Why* am I *here?*"

"*Not* the right question," she snapped and crossed her arms as she leaned against a tree of such monumental size, I couldn't see to the top of it. "I already told you that. I already answered you. And it's the only answer you're going to get to that question."

"Why are *you* here?"

"Ah, better question," the old woman nodded. She pushed her ample weight off the tree and grabbed her cane to steady herself. "Moving in the right direction. Closer to where you need to be."

Ms. Elkins shuffled toward me slowly as her watery eyes stared me down. Time seemed to slow as the old woman made her way toward me. I sensed so much from whatever presence was here besides Ms. Elkins that it was hard to keep my own thoughts straight.

It felt like I was being tested. Judged. Weighed.

The gentle breeze slowed as Ethel moved closer.

Finally, she stood directly in front of me. The breeze stopped, and the air felt heavy. The wizened old woman stared eye to eye with me. Again, her size seemed adaptable to her point.

"You are the Thirteenth Witch. We knew you were coming into being. What shall be now watches over you."

I waited for an explanation.

She did not continue.

Moments passed, and the air hung stationary waiting for something.

In a flash, the disembodied energy's impatience at the silence made it clear that everyone was waiting for me.

"What is the Thirteenth Witch?" I asked.

As soon as the words left my mouth, Ethel raised her cane above her head and twirled with it so fast I would've sworn the old woman was a prima ballerina. Pink, blue, and purple fog poured out from the old woman's twisting tornado. It flew through the air like billiard balls bouncing around the pool table.

As the ricocheting fog slowed, the pink mist coalesced into the faceless silhouette of a woman, the blue into an anonymous man. The purple mist swirled around them in a circle.

"There are two!" the old woman shouted as her frenetic turning came to a halt. "Two are the thirteenth witches. Two that must become the one. The Thirteenth Witch will release the energy that returns the power to the paranormal world. It is the shape of the world's destiny."

"I don't understand," I told Ms. Elkins as the fog figures clasped hands.

"The power was taken, and hidden! It was a *dangerous* power, and it corrupted the supernaturals. When the world changed, they did not. When the world evolved, they did not. And so it was *taken* from them!" Ethel shouted, raising her cane high in the air. Lightning seemed to shoot from her cane to the sky.

"Taken by who?"

"It is time," she said, calming. "It is time for the power to return. It is time for hope to return, for the magic to heal! For the benefit of all! It is time for the punishment to end. It all ties together. Everything ties together like the roots of a tree. When you think you have walked far from its shade, you still stand upon it. Remember that."

"What punishment? I don't understand what you're saying," I told Ms. Elkins, grabbing her arm. "You're making no sense."

"You understand enough," Ethel Elkins told me quietly, and she reached her index finger out to gently poke my forehead. "Remember when I said you could safely ignore me? Now, you can't. Keep that in mind. You understand enough, for now. You and I will meet again."

With a gentle push against my face just above my eyes, the world went black, and I felt myself falling, falling, falling into darkness…

I awoke with a scream.

CHAPTER 9

"IT FELT LIKE THE WHOLE DREAM HAPPENED IN JUST five minutes or so," I told Gunther as I poured cream into his coffee. "But it's morning, so it must've lasted all night. It's just completely bizarre."

"Time moves differently in the dream world than in our world," Gunther told me as he nodded and sipped the coffee I made. "I've never had a visitation like that, so I can't tell you what it feels like personally."

"Wait a minute, are you saying that for some reason the crazy old lady at the Makepeace Circus *literally* visited my dream to talk to me?"

"Sit down, Charlotte," Gunther said gently. He wiggled his finger and magically pulled out the dining chair to his right. Gunther's demeanor had shifted as I recounted my dream to him, starting with polite attention and ending...well, with an expression similar to my father's when he wanted to talk to me about my breaking curfew.

Gunther looked fantastic first thing in the morning, by the way. His sandy hair was disheveled, and sticking up in so many directions I'd need magic to count the directions quickly. There was a sexy, rugged stubble all over his face I desperately wanted to touch to see what it felt like.

But I didn't. We needed to focus.

"Okay, I'm sitting," I told him as I plopped down on the chair.

"Do you remember when you met Ethel Elkins for the first time? The first time you visited my circus to rescue Mark?"

The first time I visited the Makepeace Circus and the first time Gunther *remembered* I visited the Makepeace Circus were two different times. I decided not to mention that and merely nodded.

"Do you recall her telling me she wasn't crazy? That she knew more than I thought, and I should be ready?"

"Yep, I remember," I told him. "She's kinda hard to forget."

"She's been talking about the prophecy of the Thirteenth Witch for as long as I've known her," Gunther told me, taking another sip of his coffee. "To make a long story short, Ethel claims that the reason the magical circuses exist is that true paranormal power had to be hidden."

"*True* paranormal power? What does *that* mean?"

"She claims paranormals used to have the power to shape reality. Not just their own, but *all* reality. At most, now, an individual paranormal can affect themselves, maybe a couple of other people, but no one has enough magical power to, say, level a town."

"I do," I told him with more than a little ego.

"Actually, you don't," Gunther pointed out. "Your massive power stops at the borders of the Magical Midway. So does my father's."

"Well, if you want to get technical about it..."

"Technicalities are pretty important in magic, Charlotte. In any case, Ethel believes the circuses are guarding the power because it was taken away from the paranormal world."

"Why? By who?"

"Who is a paranormal mystery, I suppose," Gunther said. "She's never told me. *Why* is an easier question to answer. The paranormal world became aggressive and manipulative, and used their magic to hurt one another and the humans they were supposed to help. So the power was taken away from the paranormal world."

"But if what you're saying is true it wasn't taken out. I mean, we *have* it."

"Yes and no, and it's contained in some important ways. Remember, energy has to go *somewhere*. Ms. Elkins says it was given to the most moral, ethical, and goodhearted families in the paranormal world to guard. It was their job to hold it until the paranormal world relearned their natures, their purpose. Relearned how to be…good, I guess? Benevolent might be a better word."

"I still don't get what the Thirteenth Witch business is."

"The other part is that the energy would be withheld from the paranormal world for thirteen generations," Gunther said. "You and I, Charlotte, are our families' thirteenth generation after the founding of the circuses."

"So you and I are the thirteenth witches?"

"According to Ethel Elkins, we are."

"Well, that's cute and witchy and everything, but why does that matter?"

"What I told you up until now is history and

myth. The prophecy part is that the Thirteenth Witch will have the chance to remove the last of the immoral corruption from the paranormal world and return the power to the paranormal citizens. If the Thirteenth Witch failed, the power would disappear from the world forever."

"Wait a minute. You just said energy can't disappear."

"No, it can't, but our *access* to it can," Gunther pointed out. He clasped his mug and downed the rest of his coffee. "And all energy is connected, Charlotte. If the paranormal world's magic was a body, the magical energy animating the two circuses would be considered its heart. Once that goes, I can only guess what would go with it."

"Do you *believe* any of this?" I asked Gunther.

"I don't know," he answered after considering my question. "In the magical world, it's sometimes hard to separate truth from the myths, and even the myths may have gotten corrupted over time. What I do know is if it's true, I can't dismiss it," he said. Gunther shifted in his chair, his eyes downcast. "And Ethel foretold some other things that I can't dismiss…"

"Like what?"

"Like you."

Shivers ran down my spine at Gunther's answer even though some part of me expected it.

The night I traveled astrally to the Makepeace Circus, the old woman seemed to speak directly to me even though no one at the circus was supposed to be able to see me. Gunther didn't even know I was there and witnessed his conversation with her. It was a conversation that confused me at the time, but which now made slightly more sense, given the story my boyfriend just shared with me about the nature of Ethel Elkins.

"Ms. Elkins foretold *you*, Charlotte. That you would come from the human world, that you would need guidance. That you would be alarmed at the corruption you witnessed from the Witches' Council. That you would be a catalyst for my finding my place and becoming who I was always destined to be."

As I thought back through the experiences of the last few months, I could see how that fit me. Gunther was training me and my natural magical witch power. I had lived, mostly, in the human world before being elevated to ringmaster. Without me, Gunther would've remained a half-witch, and he might not have put on the lawgiver ring. I could see it all, and I shivered again.

"She told you all this about the next ringmaster of the Magical Midway?"

Gunther shifted uncomfortably in his chair, and his eye twitched. Without warning, he pushed away from the table. Snatching the mug, he turned away from me to put it in the sink.

And he stayed facing away from me, unwilling to turn around.

"Gunther, you're freaking me out a little."

"I'm sorry for that. I don't mean to," Gunther told the wall as I stared at his back. He sighed deeply. Without turning around, he spoke once more.

"Ethel told me all this about the woman that would become my wife."

Slow down.

Leave me alone, Samson.

We must talk.

Go. Away.

I'm not proud of the fact that I pushed away from the table so hard that the chair clattered to the floor. I will admit I'm a little embarrassed that I ran out of my own yurt while Gunther called after me. I'm a little mortified that I ran straight to the haunted house, slammed the door, and threw myself down on the couch with my legs tucked to my chest, my arms wrapped around them. While hyperventilating.

But, you know, what Gunther said was a lot to take in.

The ghosts of the house gave me a wide berth as I sat in the entryway. It was cool, and dark, and still in this place. Though I knew the ghosts were here, and I was sure they knew I was here, the absence of life was comforting.

Charlotte, we must talk, Samson insisted again.

"Get out of my head!" I shouted, cracking the stillness of the cool, lightless seating area. "I mean it, Samson. Leave me the hell alone! Give me just ten minutes to myself! Please!"

His presence slipped far enough away from me I felt like I had some breathing room. Just as Samson withdrew, a tiny glowing head popped around the archway that took patrons deeper into the house.

"Charlotte?" little Anna whispered. Her innocent eyes stared at me. "Are you okay?"

I nodded, brushing away the tears I hadn't realized had fallen. "I'm just a little overwhelmed, that's all."

"Yeah, my mommy says you have a tough job."

Anna came out from the archway and walked over to me. The little girl that looks no more than five was really two hundred and fifty-seven years old. "Maybe when I grow up I can get a job like yours."

"I don't know that you want my job, Anna." She sat down next to me. "My job seems to come with an awful lot of complications. And predetermined relationships, as it turns out."

Fiona flew in the door, breathing heavily, and stared at me. "I'm so glad you're predictable, Charlotte. I was about to turn this place upside down looking for you."

"Why? What's wrong *now*?"

"Gunther told me about your...discussion." Fiona sat on the other side of little Anna. "He also told me how you ran out the door, and he was worried about you."

"Of course he is. Why wouldn't he be? I mean, I've been preselected by the universe to be the man's wife. If he doesn't marry me, does he get assigned another one?" I asked her bitterly.

"Oh, my goodness, the most powerful witch in the entire world is feeling sorry for herself. Should I get the barbershop quartet in here to sing you a sad song? I think one of the centaurs plays the violin. We could get him in here to play it for you," Fiona snapped, rolling her eyes.

"What the heck is wrong with you?"

"Wrong with me? Wrong with *me*? Charlotte, you are my best friend in the *entire* world, and I love you, but you're acting like a complete idiot," Fiona retorted.

"Gee, Fiona, why don't you tell me how you *really* feel."

"I always tell you how I really feel," Fiona said, leaning forward. "I'm going to choose my words carefully at the moment because there are children present, but how could you treat him like that?"

"Like what? I didn't do anything to him!"

"He told you something that he's been living with since he was a *child*," Fiona pointed out. "Ethel Elkins has been telling him about his destined love since he was knee-high to a gnome. Before he knew what a girlfriend was, he was told about you. When he went to Impy and suffered through those horrible girls treating him like dirt, he dreamed about the girl that was meant for him, who would love him for who he is."

"That's really romantic," Anna said with a giggle. "It's like a fairytale!"

"It *is* like a fairytale," Fiona agreed. "Or at least

it was until Gunther opened up to the woman he's been waiting for all his life, and she ran out of the yurt crying like her puppy had just died."

"That's not fair," I told her, angry. "This was just sprung on me out of thin air!"

"*Everything* has been just sprung on you out of thin air! That's the gig, Ringmaster! If you haven't figured that out by now, take some time in this darkened hallway to come to terms with it. Because in case you didn't get the gist of Gunther's story, you *don't* have time to sit here and wallow while lamenting how unfair it is the universe decided you should have a cute blond."

"You're missing the point."

"Then explain it to me, so I don't think you're acting like a ninny."

I glared at my obnoxiously blunt friend as I tried to calm myself down. But I just couldn't.

"Fiona, what if he only cares about me because he thinks he's supposed to?" I whispered, and the tears exploded from my eyes.

Fiona jumped off her chair and kneeled down in front of me wrapping her arms around me. "Stop it. Just *stop* it. That's the most ridiculous thing I've ever heard in my life. You *know* when someone is telling the truth. You *know* when someone is genuine with you. It's why life was so hard for you in the human world. You *know* how Gunther feels about you. Prophecy or not."

"She's right! She's right she's right she's right!" Anna, who I had completely forgotten about, shrieked as she bounced up and down on the couch. "I heard him talking to Anya, and he said how much he likes you. His eyes get all googly and soft when he talks about you," she said, giggling.

"When did you hear Anya and Gunther talking?"

"Watch this!" Anna burst out. She stood up and held out her little arms. Smiling at me, I heard a pop, and little Anna disappeared. "You can't see me anymore, can you? I just learned how to do this! My mom said that ghosts used to be able to do it, but nobody could do it for years and years and years and years, but now we can all do it again!"

Her voice moved around the room as if she was racing from one corner to another, and I could sense her excited emotions and thoughts, but not even a whisper of a shadow indicated she was there.

"That's really impressive, Anna," I told her. "Can all the ghosts do that?"

"Yep, everybody can do that, but they don't

want you to know because they could be listening to people's conversations and people could get mad and...uh-oh," Anna said as her excitement level dropped. The little girl reappeared and looked up at me, concerned. "I don't think I was supposed to tell you we could do that."

"Don't worry, little one," Anna's mother said as she came through the entryway. "We don't keep secrets from our ringmaster, do we?"

"But Joe said we shouldn't tell—"

"Hush now, little one," her mother said with a stern look. "I think you said quite enough."

"Yes, ma'am." Anna pouted.

"Ringmaster," Anna's mother, bowed her head. "It's good to see you again. Fiona."

"Hello there," I said, unclenching my body from the tense ball I had been in. Standing up, I nodded and tried to actually *look* like a ringmaster. "I don't think I remember your name."

"I don't believe I actually told you the last time we met," the matronly woman said. "My name is Gerda. It's nice to meet you more formally."

"You as well, Gerda," I nodded.

"Little Anna is correct, we all have the ability to make ourselves invisible and travel outside the house without alarming anyone or risking anything," Gerda said. "It is actually good you came to visit us. Some of us have overheard things during the festival, Charlotte. Things I think you should be aware of."

"Everybody here?"

The ghosts crowded again into the front hallway. I recognized none of the faces other than Anna and her mother Gerda.

"Did we get new ghosts?"

"Why would you ask that?" a gigantic ball of a man asked as he twirled his handlebar mustache. "Don't you remember us from when you and Dergal had your...ah, discussion?"

It wasn't a discussion. It was more like an interrogation, really. And not a very successful examination if I recalled what took place in this hallway accurately.

"I don't remember you from last time."

"Ghosts can change their appearance, Charlotte," Fiona told me. "I think only Anna and Gerda look the same as before."

"I met you when I looked like this so I want to stay looking like this so you'll always recognize me!" Anna told me in a rush. "What if I waved to you and you don't know who I am and then you don't wave back? I would be *really* sad."

"Well, I definitely don't want you to be sad, Anna," I told her. The little girl giggled in response and nodded.

"I used to be the dapper, spectacled gentleman who greeted you at the door," the non-spectacled non-dapper chubby man told me. "In any case, Gerda relayed that you might be interested in some of the festival conversations that we have overheard."

"Oh yes, especially the ones that have taken place between that elf and that witch," another ghost nodded knowingly.

"Which witch?" Fiona asked.

"The dark and gloomy one that looks like she belongs in here with us," another specter chimed in from the back.

"Terrifying woman," a voice from the crowd called out.

"But very crafty, that one," someone said. The crowd murmured in agreement.

"Indigo overheard Bolt and Devana talking late last night," Gerda told me. "She came to me when she got back because she was concerned. She heard the Witches' Council mentioned."

"I did, indeed," a high-pitched voice called

from the corner near the door. "The two of them was thick as thieves, they was. She was givin' him what for, too, about the stunt he pulled with you."

"Did you get a sense of what stunt she was talking about specifically?"

"She was incredibly angry at him, wot with the draggin' you through the festival yesterday," the voice said through all the phantasms squeezed into the front hallway. I stood on my tiptoes trying to spot the ghost the voice belonged to, but I couldn't see her. "Said he was crossin' lines that he shouldn't be crossin', wot with the makin' you all woozy boozy and all."

"That doesn't make any sense," I said as I turned to Fiona.

"It does if she's running the plot, and he screwed up some plan she had," Fiona disagreed.

"She *looks* like she'd be at the center of an evil plot," someone murmured. The crowd agreed.

"What did she say about the Witches' Council?" I called in the small voice's general direction.

"Just that he knows the rules," the voice called back. "Said if he got caught breaking them, he knows exactly what will happen to him."

"What rules? Did she specifically say

something about Witches' Council rules?" Fiona asked.

"No, Miss, but who else has rules? I didn't hear much more than that."

"We need to go back and talk to my uncle."

"Why?"

"Samson told me there were things I needed to know about the huntress witch," I told her. "I just realized that my uncle was so annoyed with me that he never actually bothered to tell me them after he lectured me."

CHAPTER 10

"No," I told Gunther as I walked back into my yurt with Fiona. He had clearly been waiting for me, and he practically jumped toward me as soon as I walked in the door. "I don't have time for this, or you. I can't talk about it yet. Not now."

"Charlotte, we need to—"

"I said no."

Gunther flinched.

Fiona's eyebrows screwed up in judgment as I snapped at my…Boyfriend? Betrothed? Soon to be husband? Destined partner?

For the moment, despite Fiona's assurances that I knew Gunther's feelings were genuine, I didn't have the emotional bandwidth to confront what he had told me. He had kept it from me as I had kept Aidan's secret from Tabitha. I understood, now, even more, why Tabitha had been so angry at me.

My trust in him had wobbled. My confidence in myself was shaken. Most of all, though, I was afraid I was in a relationship that just wasn't real. That my fear about Gunther's feelings being informed by his past was more than justified. Maybe he didn't love me. He loved the me he *expected* since he was a child. He loved the *idea* of me.

Gunther's itsy-bitsy revelation little more than an hour ago had rattled me. Relationships are complicated enough without magic, circuses, and prophecies thrown in. I wish I could say the reason I was pushing Gunther away was because I was having trouble processing what he said. But that wasn't it.

Well, not entirely.

I knew I would have to ask him how long he knew before he told me, and I probably would not like the answer. Fiona seemed insistent that he known for almost as long as he'd been alive. How could he not tell me? Did he keep it from me because he knew I would see his feelings weren't real? That they were just some manufactured side effect of his belief in the prophecy?

Until I had that answer, I didn't want to talk to him about anything else. And yet…I wasn't ready to ask the question.

I wasn't sure I wanted to know.

"You wanted to talk to me?" Uncle Phil asked as he walked in. "Samson said you had some questions about Devana."

"Yeah, I do," I told him.

"Look, Mr. Astley, we're kind of in the middle of something. Could you give us a minute? You, too, Fiona," Gunther asked my uncle and friend. I glared at him and turned back to my uncle.

"We're not in the middle of *anything*. Anything Gunther and I need to talk about can wait, Uncle Phil."

"What's going on here?" My uncle looked at my boyfriend and me suspiciously. No one responded. Uncle Phil turned to Fiona, and she mouthed something that I didn't see.

"What? I can't read lips, Fiona."

Oh for heaven's sake. Charlotte found out about the prophecy as it relates to the golden boy over there, Samson told him.

My jaw dropped as *another* person I trusted admitted they had been keeping things from me.

"Are you *kidding* me? Everyone in this room knew about this prophecy that I was supposed to marry Gunther? Everyone *except* for me?"

"Wait. You're supposed to marry Gunther?" Uncle Phil asked me, confused.

"No!"

"Yes," Gunther said.

Maybe, Samson said.

Fiona wisely remained silent, and then headed out of the door.

"And that's what Ms. Elkins has told me over the years," Gunther finished explaining. Uncle Phil looked gobsmacked.

"I don't even understand how that *could* work, Gunther," my uncle said once he finished. "Far be it from me to question the prophecy of a norn, but you and Charlotte have responsibilities and limitations upon you that would make a...well, a more permanent and serious relationship quite impossible."

"I'm well aware of that."

"Does no one listen to me when I say I don't want to talk about this right now?" I asked the two men sitting in my yurt, sipping my tea, and discussing my future.

I'm not trying to interfere in your relationship, Charlotte, but... Uncle Phil trailed off. His gaze traveled from my face to Gunther's and back again. *Charlotte, I understand that you may be upset with the boy for withholding this from you on a personal level, but the tale he just told goes far beyond your feelings for him or his for you.*

"What do you mean?" Uncle Phil looked relieved that I had spoken out loud.

"The prophecy of the Thirteenth Witch is quite a bit more than a fairy tale romance, Charlotte," Uncle Phil said, shifting on his chair. "It is rumored to herald a cataclysmic change in our paranormal world. The arrival of the Thirteenth Witch is supposed to usher in an age of freedom, a return to the magic that we once had. Our return to our place as the guardians of the humans."

"I didn't know about that part," Gunther said.

"Indeed. There seem to be pieces of the story held in different places within our world. Different families, different creatures know different facets of it. Interestingly enough," Uncle Phil said, standing up. "Devana and the huntress witches are part of the myth that *I* know."

"How do you mean?"

"The huntress witches are supposed to be the guardians of morality in the paranormal world—" my uncle began.

"That woman dressed in black talking like someone that takes people down for fun is a *guardian of morality*? Are you *kidding* me?" I burst out. Everything about Devana seemed...dark. Dangerous. She didn't scream moral. Or guardian. Or safe.

"Charlotte, again, stop looking at this through human eyes, human ideas of morality," my uncle said as he leaned toward me. "Oh, no, here... Think about the myths that you learned in your human school. Those creatures and gods that brought balance, or justice, were very often the most terrifying. Not that Devana is terrifying, but her purpose in the story of the Thirteenth Witch is not an easy one."

"What purpose is that?"

"A necessary one," Uncle Phil said. "To cull those that poison the soul of the paranormal world."

"Uncle Phil, she said she *hunted* our kind! Circus people!"

"If the purpose of the nomads is to keep the energy we supposedly guard traveling around so it can't be grabbed," Gunther pointed out, "then you could reasonably assume we've had bad people taking cover in our circuses over the years, too. Think about it, Charlotte—if someone was after you, where's the best place to hide?"

"Behind an impenetrable wall that moves all over in a way no one can predict," I said.

"And with those that do not subject themselves to the normal rules," Gunther added.

"Then there's really two possibilities if Devana is who this Thirteenth Witch prophecy claims she is," I told them. "One, she's the person directing the murder of Chase Trout because he was some kind of paranormal cancer that needed to be rooted out. Someone trying to frame me is a separate issue of convenience."

"And the other?" Uncle Phil asked.

"That she's decided I'm the immoral thing that needs to be taken down, and that's why she's here. His murder was just a means to an end."

"Why would she be dating Chase Trout's brother, though?" Gunther asked.

"Maybe the prophecy made her do it." My answer dripped with sarcasm, and Gunther winced again.

None of this feels right, Samson said.

"What do you mean, it doesn't feel right?" I asked the cat.

A huntress doesn't plot. They're not conniving. Murdering someone just to catch someone else...that would be immoral. They also don't hide their actions from anyone. Nothing is secret. No one would fear to cross them if it was. If Devana had killed Chase Trout, we would know. She would not hide the how, or the why.

I related what Samson said to Gunther while my uncle tapped his fingers on the table, deep in thought.

"I need to talk to Devana," I told the assembled group.

"Are you *daft?*" my uncle asked. "Did you hear anything that I just told you?"

"Nothing you just said leads me to believe that I shouldn't talk to her. In fact, we both have a role to play in some grand prophecy. Seems like Gunther and I both *have* to talk to her."

"You want to invite her here?" Gunther asked, surprised. "You could be putting your citizens in danger. Not to mention you would scare the heck out of them."

"I didn't think about that," I agreed. Some paranormals never, ever left the safety of the Magical Midway. With this new information, I now wondered why. Could I be harboring criminals? Murderers? I shuddered.

Silence descended as all four of us sifted through the information in our minds.

I realized I had learned an incredible amount of information over the course of two days, but none of it painted a clear picture of what was going on. I remained as much in the dark about who and what was behind all this as I was when I arrived.

And time was running out.

"Okay, then break out the blue rose," I told my uncle. "If I can't bring her here, and I can't go there, I need to do some snooping. The ghosts overheard some interesting information as they wandered around."

"They did?" Uncle Phil asked.

"Yeah, they can apparently float around invisible now," I told him. "Go get your stuff out of your yurt. I want to take a walk on the invisible side."

Uncle Phil nodded, hopped up, and walked away. He turned once as if he wanted to say something else, but a second later he shrugged and left the yurt.

∿

"I'm sorry," Gunther said as soon as we were alone. His voice was soft and hesitant. Not hesitant enough to not talk about the darn thing, though, the moment we were by ourselves.

Well, we weren't alone.

Samson jumped up on the bed and curled up on my pillow. I could see his ear standing at alert on top of his head as the cat pretended to doze.

"Please, Gunther, not now," I insisted.

"I've been waiting almost twenty years to have this conversation, Charlotte," he told me as he turned to look me in the eye. "Ever since my mother died, ever since Ethel told me about this supposed destiny."

"Then a few days more or less aren't going to matter," I snapped at him and turned away.

"I need to say this now," he said, his voice growing stronger. "And I need you to hear me. You don't have to say anything. But I need you to know this, hear it, and believe it."

I paused.

I didn't want to have this conversation, but no one in this entire circus seemed to have the ability to be patient. Everything had to be dealt with right then, with no delay. With no ability to process, with no ability to wait.

As usual, I acquiesced.

"Oh, fine, what?"

"I'm sorry that I didn't tell you," he said. "But put yourself in my position. For the first time in my life, I meet someone that's beautiful, interesting, confident…and she likes me. She doesn't judge me for being a half-witch, or a nomad. She knows all sorts of things I've only heard rumors of. She loves the kind of life that I love. Charlotte, you were more than I ever could have hoped for…more than I deserved."

"Oh, Gunther, stop," I told him, my heart cracking open at his words even as I struggled to hang on to my anger at him.

He moved over to the couch and sat beside me, grabbing my hand and squeezing it. "I love you, Charlotte. And I didn't want to say anything or do anything that could push you away."

"I just can't believe that you kept that from me," I told him. "We talk about everything, Gunther. How could you not tell me about this?"

"I wanted to be sure that you really liked me," he said. "I didn't want you to wind up being with me because of some obligation. I wanted to give you the chance to make your own choice, unencumbered by the weight of all this. I felt you deserved that."

"I do like you, Gunther," I sighed. I still

couldn't say love. All the revelations still swirled like a chaotic storm in my brain, confusing me. "I just hate that all of this keeps getting sprung on me. And it makes me wonder…"

"Yes?" Gunther leaned closer.

"Well, what if you only *think* you love me? Because you know about all this stuff? What if you don't really feel about me the way you think you do? You kept this from me to ensure my feelings were genuine for you. How am I supposed to believe your feelings are genuine for me?"

"Oh, Charlotte," he laughed and leaned forward. "How could anyone not love you?"

"Well, there's the Witches' Council and—"

Gunther leaned forward to silence me with our very first kiss. I closed my eyes, stomach jumping nervously and waited.

And then I heard the metallic clunk.

"Ow," Gunther said, and I felt his weight shift away from me quickly. My eyes flew open to a surprised Gunther sporting a bloody lip.

"What happened?" I asked him in a panic.

"I, um…" he mumbled as he grabbed a napkin from the coffee table and held it to his mouth. "I think your ringmaster protection is pretty all-encompassing, Charlotte." He laughed as he pressed the napkin down harder trying to stop the bleeding.

"Wait, I don't understand," I told him, my panic rising. "You can't kiss me?"

"There may be certain kisses that are unavailable to us," he said, muffled. "Can you get me some ice, please?"

Ohmygoshyouhavetobekiddingme! I shouted in my mind to no one in particular. I jumped up and ran over to the magic refrigerator.

I explained to you that your protections operate much like a full body shield, Samson interjected. I tried to steady my shaking hands. *The full body being the operative words.*

Do you mean to tell me I can't kiss Gunther? At all?

Nope. At least not like that. A peck on the cheek should work.

I raced back to Gunther and handed him a washcloth filled with ice. He smiled and took the napkin away. This time, it was me who winced at his swollen, bloody lip.

"I am *so* sorry," I whispered, my eyes tearing up.

"Charlotte, it's not your fault. It's mine, really. I should have thought that through a bit more before I kissed you. It was my enthusiasm that got me," Gunther chirped.

"I can't believe you're taking this so well," I told him. "I feel like *I'm* going to throw up."

"It's fine, really," Gunther said, pressing the ice against his face. "Like I said, I really should have expected something like this would be in place."

"What would be in place?" Uncle Phil asked as he walked in. He looked at Gunther with the ice on his face and my stricken expression and nodded. "Ah, yes. I should have told you two about that. I didn't realize that the relationship had progressed to that point quite yet."

"You had to deal with this?"

"Oh, yes. Jeannie is quite a bit happier now than she was before. It does give a relationship a certain old-fashioned quality that could be quite charming." Uncle Phil began placing the rock and cauldron down on the floor. "At least until the sexy fun starts—"

Uncle Phil's eyes opened wide, and then he whirled around whistling.

"Why did you stop talking?" I asked him.

"Just getting ready, dear. Let me concentrate now."

Uncle Phil, what was that? What were you going to say?

Later, dear, he answered. *Perhaps now isn't the time.*

Samson, what is he hiding from me?

Your uncle is right. We can have this discussion later.

I watched my uncle setting up for my spying spirit walkabout nervously. Whatever they were hiding from me was probably obvious, but I was so rattled by bashing in Gunther's lip from a kiss that I couldn't calm down enough to think straight.

"Charlotte, I'm fine," Gunther told me. "No worries."

I worried.

I worried a whole lot.

Later, I would be grateful that I didn't piece it all together in front of my boyfriend, my uncle, and that stupid cat.

CHAPTER 11

SEPARATING FROM MY BODY THIS TIME WENT FAR quicker than the last time. I knew what to expect, and I wasn't as nervous. I heard the pop and looked down at my drooling, catatonic body glowing blue, with a sense of accomplishment.

"Is she gone?" Gunther asked Uncle Phil. His eyes grew wide. He stared at the saliva slowly creeping down the corner of my mouth. Fantastic.

"Likely so," my uncle answered, throwing more blue rose on the cauldron fire. "Charlotte can allow us to see and hear her, but it doesn't seem like she did so this time. She could still be in the room, but it's far more likely that she's already gone to see what she can find out."

Or that she's hanging out and listening to her boyfriend and uncle talk about her without telling them. That could be happening, too.

Shut up, Samson.

Oh, keep your britches on.

Not sure I can do anything other than that at the moment.

Anya and Faleena walked into my yurt laughing. "Hey, Charlotte, we came to drag you to a campfire party." Anya leaned down and grabbed my limp arm trying to tug me from the floor, but I flopped over. "Charlotte! What's wrong with her?"

"She's, um, meditating," Gunther told Anya. Faleena crossed her arms and looked on suspiciously. "We were doing a meditation exercise. She's quite good at it."

"Yes, Gunther was just showing her how to meditate. She's been a little stressed, what with the whole suspicion of murder thing at the festival," Uncle Phil agreed. My uncle reached out and grabbed my other arm to yank me back upright.

"She seems pretty relaxed to me," Anya observed.

"Yes, she is very, very deep into the

meditation," Gunther told her and coughed. "She's a quick study."

"So, Anya, why don't you stay here and wait for your friend to wake up," Faleena told her. "I'm going to head back to my campsite and change for the party. Never know who you're going to meet, you know?"

"Yeah, okay. Meet me back here?"

"I'll be back in about an hour," Faleena said as she made for the door. Her hand slipped into her pocket, and she threw something behind my table as she turned to head out the door. No one other than me spotted it, and I only saw it because it glowed and pulsed with magical energy in this alternate dimension I inhabited.

It's an eye, Samson informed me.

Oh my gosh, she just threw somebody's eye in my yurt?

Not an eye as in someone's eye, Samson responded with more than a little bit of sarcastically exaggerated patience. *An eye as in an enchanted spyglass. Whoever is at the other end of that eye can see everything that happens in this room. Well, through the chair and table legs. Faleena didn't have a very good aim.*

Can they hear anything?

Of course not. It's not an ear. It's an eye.

Tell Uncle Phil about the eye. I'm going to follow her. I knew there was something off about Faleena.

Let's leave it until you return. Just in case it's got wards, you should be the one to grab it. You have more protections than they do.

Okay.

Be careful, Charlotte.

I floated along after Faleena. The werebear had given me a few nonspecific indications there was something suspicious about her, but this was the first time it was clear she had something to hide.

Anya seemed to know the woman, and trust her, so I hadn't given Faleena much thought, despite her weird behavior and attitude. Now, I regretted that decision.

She stomped loudly behind the campsites and the more populated areas of the festival. The moonlight gave me a clear view of the crowds gathered around campfires and along the road, as well as the distance Faleena was putting between them and us.

"Are you here?" she called toward a rather large tree. Bushes shuffled, and a figure emerged from the darkness.

Scout.

"I've been waiting a half an hour for you," Scout told her. "It was almost impossible for me to shake Devana. She'll be wondering where I am."

"Here," Faleena told him, handing him another glowing rock. "It's in her tent, but I didn't get to place it well. I don't know what you're going to be able to see."

So, Scout Trout was spying on me. But why?

"There is no way I'm letting that one-eyed drunkard Wayland keep me from being elevated tomorrow." Scout grasped the eye. "At least now I'll know if those two are plotting."

Wayland and I plotting? What the heck?

"I have no doubt that she and that boy are in cahoots with the cyclops," she responded. "It's clear that she and the Makepeace heir are close… if you know what I mean. Those stupid circus people. How dare they plot against werebears?"

Well, I guess I found where the accusations were originating.

"When do witches need a reason to plot?" Scout asked her. "They all think they are better than us."

"At least you know that we, your werebears, are loyal to you, future clan leader. We will not let the witches threaten our community. You would do well to push your own pet witch away from you, though, before the ceremony."

As I hovered next to the two of them and listened to the conversation they thought was private, I was even more confused.

"Devana has never given me any indication that she does not care for me," Scout growled. "She is not like the others, and holds no loyalty to the Council. You overstep your bounds, bear. You have no say over who I share my cave with."

"Don't say I didn't warn you when that huntress witch turns on you," Faleena rolled her eyes. "I will continue to stay by the side of Anya to observe the Magical Midway unless there is something else you want me to do," Faleena told him.

"No, thank you, Faleena. I appreciate your loyalty," Scout reached out to pat her on the head. "One more day and this will all be over." Scout turned and ran away from her without waiting for her response.

"He's got *that* right," Faleena mumbled. She walked deeper into the forest to another clearing some distance away. I watched the werebear sit down on a fallen log. Every once in a while she lifted her head and looked to the right and left as if she was waiting for someone.

After fifteen minutes, who that someone was became clear.

"What news have you?" Bolt emerged silently into the clearing.

"The witch is meditating. Devana is unaware of anything, as far as I know."

"And Wayland?"

"Drunk, I presume. He may be the only person at this entire festival truly grieving over that clod."

"Not even the clod's brother?" Bolt asked her politely.

"How would *I* know?"

"Did you not just meet with him?"

Faleena stared at the elf. I didn't see her move at all, but her energy changed from calm to defensive.

"I may have agreed to your plan, Faleena, but you are mistaken if you think my trust in you is unquestioning. I do not wish to be the last one standing should this all fall apart."

"You have your ring, elf. That was the only condition I needed to fulfill. Honesty and forthrightness wasn't part of our bargain.

Informing you of any other activities I engage in certainly wasn't."

"It's all right. It's not as if I would trust anything you said in any case."

"Oh, boo hoo," Faleena told him and stood up. "How you feel about me after this is of no consequence. Only my service to the Council matters. Did you come here just to be your standard charming self, or are you here to give me information?"

"It's a shame there is so much mistrust among those embarking on this little endeavor," Bolt told her. "Your rule of us was never coated in this much deception."

"Half of the people on this endeavor don't even know they're on this endeavor, you idiot. There can't be anything *but* mistrust."

"It doesn't matter to me at this point," Bolt told her, tossing back his white-blond hair. "I have what I was meant to have out of this at long last."

"I can't believe you did all this for a ring."

"I did all this for a *future*," Bolt snapped at her. "Those naiads took everything from me. And that stupid witch allowed Alexa to walk back onto the Magical Midway as if she had never stolen anything from me. None of the choices presented to me were difficult."

It was clear at this point that my suspicion about Bolt was right. Despite his actions, I could understand his anger. What Alexa had done to him—leaving him, taking his ring, stealing everything he owned in the world, and then selling it to an Impy witch for even more—was brutal.

It didn't make anything he did right.

"You seem to have a knack for intrigue, Bolt," Faleena told him.

"All elves do, when needed," he told her.

"If elves and witches were in charge of the world it would certainly be more entertaining. Unfortunately for you, elf, witches are in charge and witches will remain in charge," Faleena responded.

Bolt tilted his head and considered her statement. Then he shrugged.

"In any case, it appears that no one is the wiser at this point. We simply must run out the clock until midday tomorrow," Bolt said. "Charlotte Astley will be off at the prison with Alexa, and Wayland will be out of Scout's hair. Once he's elevated, there should be no more problems from the werebears. The

Witches' Council can run roughshod over the community as is their desire with no more interference from anyone with a spine."

"And Gunther?" Faleena asked him. "It is important that both are neutralize. Both circuses must be weakened. Roland Makepeace will crawl into a bottle once his precious son joins his wife in the great beyond. No more heir, no more circus."

"You leave that half-human weakling to me."

I rubber-banded back into my body with a *whomp*!

"Faleena!" I gasped, scrambling off the floor. "I…wait a minute."

I ran behind the dining room table and scoured the wall until I spotted the small rock Anya's friend had tossed there. With a stomp, it shattered.

"Charlotte, are you all right?"

"Yeah, there was an eye in the corner," I told Gunther. I leaned over and looked at the sparkling dust on the floor.

"An eye? You mean like a spyglass?"

"Yeah, Samson knew that it was there. You didn't tell them?"

I didn't want them to begin acting suspicious, or for whoever was spying to know it was discovered until you returned with more information. Besides, what was anyone going to see in this yurt, anyway? You drooling on the floor with your uncle and your boyfriend watching you? Not exactly exciting.

"Faleena is involved with this," I told them, glancing at Anya to gauge her reaction. "I followed her into the woods, and she met with Bolt and Scout. Well, Scout first. Then Bolt."

"Did you overhear their conversations, Charlotte?"

"I did, both of them, but honestly I can't make sense of them," I told Uncle Phil as I sat down. "Scout said he had to shake Devana to meet with Faleena, and then they talked about who was plotting against him, but then when he left Bolt showed up. It seemed like the two of them were plotting against Scout, maybe, and us for certain. The two conversations seem diametrically opposed to one another."

"There's no way that Faleena is involved in this," Anya said crossing her arms. "I've known her for years. Forget that I've known her for years, actually. She's a *werebear*. She would be banished from the entire clan if she were involved in something like this."

"Well, something like what, Charlotte? What's the plot?" Gunther asked.

"The goal is that Scout gets elevated," I told him. "That you and I are out of the way, that both circuses are weakened. The only things I know for sure are that Scout was spying on us to make sure we weren't plotting with Wayland, he thinks Faleena is working *with* him, he's concerned Wayland is working *against* him so he can't be elevated, and he didn't want Devana to know that he was going to talk to Faleena."

"And Bolt?"

"Well, Bolt hates me because I let Alexa back onto the Magical Midway. Which is fair, I guess. I mean, I understand why he's upset."

"Charlotte, focus, please," Uncle Phil said with a pained look.

"Right, sorry. He got his one ring back, and he was given it back in order to do whatever it is he's doing. Faleena knows about his ring."

"How would Faleena know about his ring?" Anya asked.

I shrugged.

"And what is he doing?" Uncle Phil asked me,

snapping his fingers toward my face to get my attention.

"Bolt seems to be working with her to ensure Gunther and I are out of the way. Bolt said all he needs to do now is run out the clock to midday tomorrow, and Scout should be elevated. Faleena reminded him he needed to take out Gunther. Then everything's done."

"Did he say anything about Chase Trout? Anything that indicates he knew who the murderer was?"

"Honestly, Gunther, I didn't get the sense that he cared about the murderer or what was going on with the werebears at all. He was much more focused on me and you."

"Wonderful. Did you get any sense of what I need to watch out for?"

"He basically said he was going to 'take care of' you, as in permanently. He didn't elaborate how, and as soon as he made the threat, I raced back here to tell you all."

Gunther paced. Uncle Phil watched him, and Anya sat silently.

"Charlotte, I'm so sorry that I brought Faleena to meet you," Anya said quietly. "I feel like my sisters and I are always causing you problems."

"This isn't your fault, Anya. Bolt and Faleena

both have been known for years to everyone here," I told her. "And your sister wasn't your fault, either."

"Yet again, suddenly, there are drama and plots seemingly out of nowhere," Gunther murmured. "But what if it's not out of nowhere? Has there been anything that's happened in the past few months that didn't have the Witches' Council's fingerprints all over it?"

"Why would the Witches' Council want Chase Trout dead?" I asked them. "And is there really no one in here that thinks the names Chase and Scout Trout for bears isn't the least little bit funny? Not even a little?"

"Stop that, Charlotte, that's disrespectful," Uncle Phil told me.

My uncle was right, but it had been killing me not to say something. I had werelion named Leo, and a Sphinx that spoke in rhymes. Why *not* call a bear Chase Trout?

"Sorry. Look, the Witches' Council was talked about multiple times in the course of the conversation I overheard between Faleena and Bolt. It could have been just a political reference? But I don't think it was."

"What do you think?" Uncle Phil asked.

"I think it's the same thing as it always is," I

told him. "I think the Witches' Council arranged all of this, and it seemed to me Faleena was the person conducting the entire conspiracy."

"Are you saying you think Faleena murdered Chase?"

"If Scout didn't, and Devana didn't and Wayland didn't and Bolt couldn't, who else could it be?"

"Are we sure that Wayland has nothing to do with this?" Gunther asked me.

"Nothing I sensed from him and nothing they said about him in that clearing gives me any indication whatsoever that he's a part of any of the conspiracies," I said.

I don't believe so, either, Samson agreed.

"Samson says he doesn't think so," Uncle Phil told the non-telepathic group.

"Then I think we need to have a conversation with Wayland. I realize that he's defensive, but we've barely spoken to him since that first day, and he hasn't sought any of us out at all, even though he's looking into what happened to his friend," Gunther said. "That means he not only knows that Charlotte didn't do it, it also means he doesn't think we have any information that's useful to him."

"Well, that's kind of offensive," I pointed out. "We are the lawgivers after all."

"I don't think so, Charlotte. I think if we let him know what we know it might make him open up to us with what he's learned. Maybe together, we can all figure out what the true motivation is behind all of this."

CHAPTER 12

GUNTHER AND I LEFT THE YURT. HE WAS INSISTENT that Wayland would be more receptive to our questions if we didn't go stalking through the festival like a mob looking for him.

"Hey, I have a question to ask you," I said as we hiked down the dirt road.

"Shoot."

"What is Ethel Elkins?"

"Ethel Elkins? The old lady from my circus?" he asked. "She's a norn. She's very old and has trouble walking. Honestly, I don't know where she came from. She's just kind of always been there."

"I mean circus-wise. What does she do?"

"Ethel? Um…nothing, really. She's a norn.

She's just herself. She doesn't really do anything formally at the circus."

"I didn't realize that you guys had folks that just lived on the grounds without taking on a role or job."

"Only Ethel," Gunther said. "Normal rules don't really apply to norns, though. People are pretty afraid to cross them. They're huge, and they foretell a person's destiny. Some say they can affect it, too, but I don't know that for sure."

The dream I had the other night kept popping up in my mind. What the old woman said at the end, about everything tying together. No matter how much I pushed it away, her words kept circling back like the dream was trying to tell me something that I wasn't hearing.

"In good ways or bad?"

"I guess that depends on your perspective." Gunther smiled. "Hey, that's Wayland's cabin. The small one with the shield on it that has the ramps in front. Well, it used to be Chase's. I guess no one's worrying about guarding Wayland."

"You think she would talk to us?"

He nodded. "Ethel Elkins? Sure, I don't see why not. She likes me. What made you think of this?"

"I don't know, really. Just that dream I had the

other night. I guess now that I'm over the shock of it I'm trying to understand what she was trying to tell me."

Gunther nodded but said nothing more. He and I had gotten to a better place since my meltdown. I think he feared to make me defensive again by continuing to talk about the dream.

Gunther and I walked toward the small cabin. Glancing around the fairgrounds, I noticed this area had tons of these small cabins all over the place, each decorated with different bear carvings. "They're awfully small for bears to stay in. Are they bigger on the inside?"

"No, why?" Gunther asked.

"Well, our yurts are huge inside, but the outside looks normal. The inside can contain little villages or big rooms and stuff. I wondered if bear shifters have that same kind of ability. These seem incredibly small for people to live in."

"How much room do you really need for a one-week festival?" Gunther answered as we drew closer to Chase's.

"Here we are." Gunther stepped back and held his arm out politely to allow me to go first. Very quaint and old world charming, that Gunther.

I stepped up and knocked on the door.

"Go away!" screeched someone from within the house. The voice was distinct, and definitely not Wayland Black's. "I got nothing to say to anyone today! Unless you're bringing brandywine, go away!"

"That's not Wayland," Gunther said turning.

"No, but the voice sounds familiar," I told him as I wracked my brain to place it. "I've heard that voice before."

"Of course you have. We were *just* talking about her."

"What are you talking about?"

"That's Ethel Elkins."

With all of the weird things that have happened since I became the ringmaster of the Magical Midway, an old woman popping up where she shouldn't be, just two minutes after I thought of her and asked about her shouldn't be that big of a deal. It's a weird coincidence, maybe, but one that could have just as easily happened in the human world. No magic involved. Just odd.

My stomach, however, raced down through my legs to wrap itself around my ankles. The coincidence was mind-boggling.

"Mrs. Elkins? It's Charlotte Astley and Gunther Makepeace. We were stopping by to talk to Wayland, and I understand he's staying here in

Chase Trout's cabin," Gunther called through the closed door.

"Are you deaf, boy? I said go away!" It sounded like cabinets slammed from within the little house, and the small structure shook with the force.

"I thought you said she was a little old lady? It sounds like someone loosed a gorilla in there."

"Ethel's a bit tougher than she looks," Gunther responded. He stepped up and knocked on the door. "Ms. Ethel, come on now. We won't bother you long. Charlotte and I really need to talk to Wayland. Is he in there?"

The door swung open, and I gasped.

"You two kids don't listen at all, do you?" the old woman squawked. She filled the door frame.

"You're the one that's not supposed to be in here, Ms. Elkins," Gunther informed the old lady politely.

"Says who? You think you know so much, Gunther Makepeace. Let me tell you, you don't know *squat*," she grumbled and waved us into Chase Trout's old cabin.

"What are you doing here, ma'am?" I asked her as I closed the door behind me.

"It's all a matter of life and death," she whispered, her voice dropping low. "The thirteenth witches will *know* this. If they do not know it now, they will know it soon enough."

"Mrs. Elkins—"

The gigantic old lady held up her hand, demanding silence. She glanced to both of us, her eyes softening. Ethel's gnarled fingers caressed my cheek, then Gunther's.

"You two are idiots," she said. Coughing, she banged her cane on the wooden floor with a loud thwack. "You are, unfortunately, the only two idiots we paranormals have in this little prophecy. So I work with what I've got."

"I don't understand what you're talking about, and if you're going to keep calling me an idiot, frankly, I don't know that I'm gonna bother trying," I told her, crossing my arms.

"Snippy, snippy, snippy," the old woman cackled. She squinted at me. "Looks like I should have picked the Magical Midway instead of the Makepeace Circus to park my rear at. Though to be fair, no one would have believed that Roland would have outlasted Phil, what with all the drinking and angst. Can't see the future perfectly all the time. Sometimes we *guess!*"

"Gunther, what the heck is she talking about?"

"I don't know, actually," he said, confused. "Ms. Elkins, what are you talking about?"

The old woman's eyes widened as she froze.

"Not yet," she said emphatically, her cane hitting the floor. Wobbling across the room, she grabbed Gunther and me by the arms and shoved us with some force toward the door. "You were looking for Wayland. Go do that. Now."

"I am so confused," I muttered as Ethel shoved me against the door frame.

"Ms. Elkins—" Gunther began, but the old woman whacked him. He stared at her, shocked, and we all froze at the door, staring at one another. I could hear Gunther's breath, and the old woman wheezing. A shout echoed from outside the open door.

Ethel Elkins nodded and patted our cheeks simultaneously one last time. She remained in silence for a few moments more, and then she nodded again. With a deep breath, she spoke one last time.

"What is happening must happen. I cannot help you. I'll be back when I can. Now go, both of you. Go do what you were doing."

She nodded to us both, shoving us out and closing the door in our faces.

～

"What *the heck* was that?" I asked Gunther as I stared at the closed door.

"Norns can be a little confusing sometimes."

"A *little* confusing? There was no purpose to any of that!"

"Oh, there *was* a purpose." Gunther pointed toward a fire twenty feet away from the cabin. "You can absolutely be assured that there was a purpose to it. Nothing a norn does is without a purpose. Come on. Let's go look for Wayland."

"No need," a gruff voice called distantly from the darkness. "I'm right here."

"Wayland? It's Gunther and Charlotte," Gunther called toward the trees. We walked around the cabin toward the voice and found Wayland in a lounge chair drinking beer from a can. He was alone, staring into a campfire that had long since gone out. The ashes were piled high and cold.

"What do you two want? Shouldn't you be enjoying your last day together?" Wayland belched and threw the empty can toward the firepit. He reached behind him, and I heard another can echo in the quiet clearing as it opened. "They seem pretty determined to make sure you go down tomorrow, heat merchant."

"I didn't do anything to your friend, so I don't

plan to go down for anything," I told him. "We wondered if you had found out anything."

"Oh, I found out a lot of things," he said. The big man took a long chug off the beer can and burped loudly again. "Your elf is a snake. Well, not a real snake, but a—"

"We get your meaning."

"Yeah, I bet you do. I hear you got issues with snakes. Water, if I remember correctly."

"Wayland, come on," Gunther said, sitting down on the foot of the chaise. "You can give Charlotte guff when we solve this case."

"Guff? Okay, boy scout, have it your way," he said. "Chase was killed. Someone stabbed him with a tree branch. His brother's an idiot, but I don't think he plotted to kill his brother. Your elf snake is trying to frame your girlfriend for the murder. There. There's what I know."

"What does Faleena Hobb have to do with any of it?" I asked him. "Or Devana?"

"What are you talking about? Those women have nothing to do with nothin', girl."

"Are you sure?"

"I'm drunk," the man responded, and belched in my direction. The scent of beer infused with some herb permeated the air around me, and I breathed out quickly to keep from gagging. "Sure? No. Drunk? Sure am."

"Look, Mr. Black, I understand that you're going through a tough time. But your friend Chase trusted you to be his executor or whatever the official paranormal title is," I told the sullen, drunk cyclops. "If that's all you know, we may not be able to figure out what's behind this. And if we can't figure out what's behind it, Chase's murderers may succeed."

Gunther reached out and gently tapped my hand. He looked at me with one eyebrow raised, and I nodded, giving him permission to tell Wayland what we knew.

"Charlotte heard Faleena talking with Bolt and with Scout."

"When?" Wayland asked Gunther.

"An hour ago, maybe two," he answered. "She, meaning Faleena, didn't talk to them at the same time. But her conversation with Bolt clearly indicated that she was part of whatever conspiracy he's engaged in."

"What we can't figure out is whether the issue with people framing Charlotte has to do with Chase's murder, or if it just presented an opportunity for someone to kill two birds with one stone," I explained.

"You'd have to have a perfect aim to kill two birds with one stone," the cyclops answered. He fell silent and looked intently into the fire that wasn't there. After a few moments passed, he spoke again. "I know I'm not as smart as you ringmasters and all, but you're both lawgivers. Why not just do that lawgiver hocus-pocus on her? Doesn't she have to tell you?"

"I'm currently suspected of being the murderer," I told him. "If I get her to confess, no one will believe it."

"And there's been some indication that I...um, well, that I may be in some danger," Gunther added. "If we make a move against Faleena out in the open, whoever's working with her could simply try and kill me."

"Can't you protect him at the Magical Midway? Isn't that the whole reason your Daddy doesn't mind you going there? That your little girlfriend can protect you?"

"How do we get her there?" I asked. "And what about Devana?"

"What about her?"

"Are they in it together?"

"No," Devana said, stepping out from behind a tree. "No, they are not. Though considering how *loudly* the three of you are speaking, if someone *wanted* to conduct a conspiracy the last thing they should do is tell you."

The severe woman seemed to reflect the moonlight with a radiance that didn't quite look natural but wasn't quite magical, either. It was as if the air around her absorbed the silver-white light and incorporated it into her skin.

"May I approach?" she asked.

I answered no as the two men agreed.

Great.

Gunther and I stood in the darkened clearing as Devana strolled toward us. She stepped through the forest with a majestic beauty that made my breath catch in my throat.

"The forest told me of your spirit walk, ringmaster," Devana told me once she drew close. "I wondered if you were the one I was sent here to protect. When the trees told me that you had emerged, I knew it was time for me to reveal myself for your protection. Please forgive my subterfuge of yesterday. I did not wish the conspirators to know my motivations in being here."

My muscles tensed. I felt Gunther tense at

almost precisely the same time next to me. What my uncle had said about the huntress witches ran through my head as tingles ran down my spine. I had to admit, her claim she was here to protect me somehow intrigued me.

On the other hand, a whole lot of people and a whole lot of things in the paranormal world seem to be precisely the opposite of what they claimed, so I wasn't taking any chances.

I stepped back when she was five feet away. Devana respectfully paused her approach.

"What do you mean, reveal yourself?" Gunther asked.

"What do you mean the trees told you?" I asked.

Devana smiled.

"As you have no doubt realized, there are many types of witches," she said. I nodded even though I really hadn't realized anything of the sort. "I am of the wild witches. I owe my allegiance to nothing but nature, and I am one of the last of the witches that keep to the balance."

"The balance of what?"

"The balance of everything," she replied. "People fear us, it is true, but they only fear us because they do not understand."

"Well, *I* don't understand," I told her. "Let's

start at the beginning. And if possible, could we leave out the cryptic statements? I'm getting enough from Ethel Elkins on that score. Just talk to me plainly. What are you here to protect me from?"

"I am here to provide the balance," she answered. "You are engaged in a war, though you may not yet realize it."

"Oh, *believe* me, I realize it."

"No, Charlotte Astley, I don't believe you do," Devana answered. She gestured to the chairs surrounding the firepit. As Gunther and I sat down, she waved her hand and roared the fire to life. "The Thirteenth Witch has been foretold to bring balance to our world. To bring down those that are too high, and to bring up those that have fallen too far."

"And I'm the Thirteenth Witch?" I asked.

"That…that answer is more complicated than you might believe. And for now, that answer is no. It is the prophecy and the steps leading to its fulfillment that you must worry about. We are early on the path."

"What happens if the prophecy is fulfilled?" Gunther asked.

"Why, balance, young Makepeace. Even your

family name cloaks you in the weight of the prophecy and your role in it."

"His name?" I asked her. "What does his family name have to do with it?"

"Not just his, both of yours. The Astley name is believed to derive from the seventh-century phrase meaning farm or settlement. The Makepeace name retains its origins, originally given to mediators. Its meaning is right in the two words that make up the whole. You see? Balance."

"While this is all really interesting," I told her, losing patience, "none of this seems particularly relevant to the situation at hand. Maybe at some point after this, I'll grab a Magic 8-Ball, shake it, and ask it what I should do. For the moment, though, I don't care about any of this. I care about who killed Chase."

"Chase was killed because he would not bring his clan out of balance," Devana leaned forward. "The bear leader was strong, and he would not yield to those that would strip his people of their culture. He was killed for it."

"How do you know that?" I asked sharply.

"I am one with the wild things. They know what happens in their forest. They see many things that we do not."

"So, the trees solve the murder, and they know who did it?"

"Trees do not have names, and so they do not know names. Chase's blood ran red along the trunk of a great tree, and the great tree knew his pain and regret at the end."

"What was his regret?" Wayland asked gruffly.

"One was that he would not see his friend before he went," Devana told the cyclops. Her voice was thick with sympathy for the man, and she answered him gently. It surprised me. "The tree said his blood ran true for you, and you were in his thoughts and in his heart. You will no doubt see your friend again, for he will wait for you."

Snot-filled snorts filled the air as Wayland choked back his grief for Chase.

"That he could not avoid his death was another," Devana told all three of us. "He was not ready to go, and he was upset with himself that he underestimated his enemy."

"Who is his enemy? Did he know?"

"Can you not guess? Who would be powerful enough to arrange the murder of one so loved? Who would benefit from turning paranormal clan against paranormal clan? Who would celebrate seeing the death of a beloved leader?"

"The Witches' Council," Gunther said.

"But why? Why would they do this? And who here works for them?" I asked.

"You already know," Devana told me. "You eliminated everyone but me and one other. If I am not the murderer, then…"

"Faleena." Gunther looked stricken at the idea of yet another friend that turned into an enemy.

"But why? Why would a werebear kill their own leader?"

"Why indeed?" Devana asked. "You have asked to set aside the prophecy of the Thirteenth Witch, and so I will say no more on the subject. I hope you understand that as the fulfillment steps ever closer, there are those that work to push it away. It is all connected."

I stared at her sharply. She stared back calmly.

"Charlotte?" Gunther asked. I knew what he was asking me. What did I sense from the strange woman? Was she telling the truth, or was this all another elaborate ruse?

In talking with Devana, my suspicion of her had slowly melted away. Her energy was…regal. Divine, almost. She had a priest-like aura about her as we spoke. Her motives and her words were clear as a still lake. There was no guile about her at all, and her emotions were uncomplicated.

Service to purpose. Care. Resolution.

"When we first met, it felt like you were hiding something from me. Now, it doesn't," I told her. "I want to trust you but…"

Your suspicion is warranted in the situation you're in, ringmaster. Hopefully, as we get to know each other better, you will learn to trust in me. I mean you no harm so long as you mean our community no harm."

"I want to believe you."

"Truthfully, it does not matter whether you believe me or believe in me. The Thirteenth Witch prophecy is coming to pass, and I am destined to play a role in it. I am destined to be at your side to keep the balance," Devana smiled.

"What if I tell you I don't want your help? That I don't believe in any of this?"

"That leaf on that tree doesn't believe in photosynthesis," Devana said, gesturing behind her to one of the towering trees in the forest. "It is, however, still green."

"Point taken," I told her.

"What's photosynthesis?" Gunther asked me.

"I really need to get the Internet at the Magical Midway," I told him.

"I would suggest that we conclude this meeting and continue with your task, Charlotte."

Devana stood up. The elegant and fierce-looking woman extended a hand to help me out of my chair.

As I clasped it, my palm grew warm, and an orb of light flashed out from our joined hands. I struggled to let go, but Devana held me firmly in her grip as the white sphere stretched out over our hands and then grew bigger and bigger and lighter until it seemed to fade.

As the light faded, I withdrew my hand. Calmly.

Coldly.

"Charlotte, are you all right?" Gunther asked me, concerned.

"Of course. A paradigm-twisting thing just happened without my knowing," I told him as I shrugged. "That's all. I should just start my day assuming that some earth-shattering paranormal event that shifts my world on its axis will take place, and most days I doubt I would be disappointed. It's just Thursday."

I turned and walked away from the three of them toward the Magical Midway so no one could see my hands shaking. Despite my dispassionate comment to Gunther, gripping the hand of the huntress witch had exploded energy within me that was racing through my veins.

Gunther's confession.

Another murder.

Another betrayal.

And another betrayal.

And now some supernatural bonding with a woman I barely had a conversation with, and certainly didn't trust. A woman I suspected of murder not an hour ago.

I walked faster as my hand shook even more.

I didn't have the energy anymore to bother with concern over a ball of light. I didn't have the power to be concerned about my future husband, the future of the circus, the future of the paranormal world, or who killed the bear leader.

The weight of it all hung over me, and I tried to shake it off. But I couldn't. As the energy raced through my veins, my resentment burned with it, a fire that exploded within me as my life was twisted one more time down a path not of my own choosing. Toward a destiny out of my hands.

Things have just changed, Samson said as my foot touched the circus ground.

Things sure have changed, Samson. I'm done.

You are what?

Done. I'm just done.

CHAPTER 13

I WANTED A EUREKA MOMENT.

Just one perfect moment where I felt everything was okay.

I wanted a moment where I figured everything out, everything clicked, everything was understood. I wished to stand up during this festival and tell everyone why Chase Trout had to die, why Faleena had probably killed him, and how they were being used by the Witches' Council in blaming me.

I wanted to fix it. And then I wanted everything to be okay. The bears would shake my hand. We'd head off to the next circus. The humans would come back and laugh. I would walk my midway knowing that this boring, nomadic life with these crazy people was secure.

No prophecies. No destinies. No secrets.

I wanted that more than anything.

This whole situation, the whole convoluted plot, the entire festival, the entire crime...It was just elaborate and *stupid*. It was one more attempt by the Witches' Council to control the paranormals they decided they would rule.

A control they would kill to keep.

Are you sure that Faleena is the one that killed Chase?

Pretty sure, although I still don't know why. And honestly, I'm starting to not care. This isn't my problem.

You're a lawgiver.

I'm an idiot. I never should've agreed to become ringmaster, and I never should've put on that stupid lawgiver ring. I'm tired of all this, Samson. Prophecies, Thirteenth Witches, ringmasters. People I thought I knew betraying me. This is all just ridiculous. It's ridiculous!

"Charlotte, are you okay? You look like you've seen a ghost."

"Yeah, let's not forget the ghosts," I told Anya as she met me walking along the path toward my yurt. "Sorry, was just having a mental conversation with the cat."

Wow, you do sound frustrated. I'm the cat again, am I?

"This imbroglio is stretching my last nerve, Anya," I told her as we walked closer to my yurt. "I think I'm done. Actually, I think I'm cracking up a little bit. Like, my mind's gone, my emotions have left the building. This is a dream, right?"

"What's been a dream?"

"Everything! Everything has to be a dream. I bet I'm not even a witch. I bet I'm some human girl having a fever dream because I'm in a hospital and I'm really sick, and the drugs are making me cuckoo," I told her, laughing. "This is bananas! A huntress witch fated to protect me, a man I turned into a witch prophesied to be my husband, a whole festival of bears that hate me because an elf got me drunk. Only I can't get drunk. And I can't kiss my boyfriend! I just…This is crazy. This is absolutely crazy!"

Charlotte, you must take a deep breath and calm down, my uncle's voice echoed in my head. *I'm heading over to you now. Don't do anything rash.*

"I shouldn't do anything rash? Are you kidding? Nothing in this stupid place is anything other than rash!" I shouted to the entire Magical

Midway. People milling about left and right stopped to stare. I glared at all of them and laughed again. "What? Like you people act so normal? Go stare at someone else!"

Anya was stupefied as Gunther raced up to us.

"Charlotte, you're making a scene. Come on, let's go inside," he said, grabbing my arm.

"It's my ridiculous circus, isn't it? I can make a scene if I feel like it. And I have to tell you, husband to be, I really feel like it!"

"Then get the heck over it!" Ethel Elkins said as she stomped up on the three of us. "You're a grown woman! Get a hold of yourself!"

I stared at the norn glaring down at me and burst into peals of laughter. Tears rolled down my face as the tension wracking my body tried to expel itself through any release available.

"I don't know what I'm supposed to do," I whispered to her through maniacal laughter I couldn't entirely control.

"No, you don't know what you're supposed to do! And you're trying to figure it out alone," the old woman answered sternly. "If you keep recoiling from every hand extended to you, every aid sent to you by fate, you will lose your mind, and this fight!"

"Balance, Charlotte," Devana said as she

walked up calmly. "You are overwhelmed because you feel that you are alone. I ask you, sister, how could one such as you *ever* be alone? Think, Charlotte. Breathe in the scent of the forest, the air of your home, and think."

I can't think. I can't breathe.

You can. We are here, all of us, to help you, Samson said.

As I felt Samson reach across the Magical Midway to give me an anchor in my emotional storm and slam control around me, I glanced sheepishly around at the eyes watching me with concern. Turning, I raced into my yurt for privacy.

I wanted to apologize to them for my outburst, for making the citizens of the Magical Midway nervous yet again, but I wasn't sorry. I had finally come unglued, and I didn't want to apologize for it.

It was all too much.

No one was speaking.

Uncle Phil, Gunther, Samson, Anya, and Devana had been joined by Fiona and Ningul. The seven of them fanned out around me as I sat in my favorite chair, sipping tea carefully while my hands continued shaking. I could see the stolen glances between them, the looks of concern. Just as I was about to speak, Ethel Elkins stomped in.

"Good, everyone is here, and she's not acting like a basket case. That means we can move on to the next phase, yes?"

"What are you talking about?" I asked her, my voice hoarse.

"I have been waiting for you to join with the huntress," Ethel said as she waved her cane in Devana's direction. "Now that you have, things are going to get a lot more complicated. I need you to pull it together."

"Ms. Elkins, perhaps now is not the time," Gunther told her respectfully.

"There is no other time, boy. This is the time. This is the time that was foretold in the time that must be," Ethel snapped at him. "You should know that."

Gunther hung his head.

"Who is this woman?" Uncle Phil asked. The others murmured the same question.

"I am the old woman that's going to save your butts," she told Uncle Phil, making her way loudly over to him and looking down into his face.

"More importantly, who the heck are you? Aren't you supposed to be dead?"

"I am dead," he told her politely.

"Well, then, shut up. This conversation concerns the living."

"Well, I never..."

"Maybe if you had, you wouldn't be dead," she snapped. "Listen up, children, because I'm only gonna say this once. Devana and I will be joining your rustic little nomadic circus. So will Gunther, at least for now—"

"Now, wait a minute, he can't—"

"He can, and he is," Ethel told Uncle Phil, cutting off whatever argument he would make.

"Don't I have to approve who joins the circus or not, as a ringmaster? Isn't there some kind of petition and binding ceremony or something?"

"Not in this case, Charlotte," Devana told me. "We three are already bound to the Magical Midway through—"

Ms. Elkins slammed her cane down on my coffee table and glared at Devana. Ouch. That would leave a mark.

"Who's telling the story, you or me? Do you speak for fate now?"

"My apologies, your Holiness." Devana bowed her head.

"I am so confused," Fiona said.

"You and me both," Anya agreed.

"In just a month's time, you will have to attend the Witches' Council meeting. We have little time to prepare, and the easiest way to do so is if the three of the balance are here," Ethel said.

"So, you, Devana and Gunther are the three?" I asked.

"Did I say that?"

"Well, no, but—"

"Stop asking questions and listen," Ethel snapped. "I'm an old woman and it's way past my bedtime. We can't do this all night. For one, I have to sleep, and two, Faleena Hobb is on her way here."

Gunther jumped out of his chair and headed for the door. "What is she coming here for?" he asked Ethel over his shoulder.

"I don't care!" I shouted. "I don't care why she's coming here. Don't you understand? Did any of you bother to listen to me before? I can't do this anymore!"

"Oh, not this again," Ethel murmured. She shuffled to the couch and plopped down. "Okay, go on. Have another meltdown. We certainly have time for you to freak out just a little more. Nothing else going on. Please, go ahead."

"Come on," Fiona said as she grabbed my hand.

"Where do you think you're taking her?" Ethel snapped as she brandished her cane like a weapon in Fiona's direction.

"I'm getting a little tired of people I don't know coming in here and thinking that they have a right to boss my friend around," Fiona told her, dropping my hand and advancing on the old woman. "Now, I'm not going to even *pretend* to understand any of this prophecy garbage, but I *can* see that my friend—who I've known, by the way, since well before any of you people showed up—is about to break!"

"Fiona, you don't understand—" Uncle Phil said.

"I understand you're all making Charlotte crazy. So back off. Give her a break."

"The kelpie means Charlotte no harm," Devana said.

"Lady, you're lucky I don't clobber you where you stand. I certainly don't need some woman that looks like she walked out of a horror movie to tell everybody that I, who have known Charlotte since we were girls, don't mean her any harm," Fiona told her.

"Devana, we know that. It's just that Charlotte—"

"Needs her friend," Devana said with finality. "It is not yet the hour of destiny, and we can spare them a moment of privacy."

"Follow me," Fiona said, grabbing me again.

I followed her out the door into the night.

"Here," Fiona said, opening the door to Ningul's log cabin within the centaur yurt. "The kelpie tent has no privacy at all. Ningul won't mind. I'm practically living here, anyway."

As I looked around, it was easy to see Fiona's touches in the decor. Her favorite flowers, white roses, were in vases all over the living room. Her sweater was flung across the couch. Were Ningul and Fiona living together? Had I become so wrapped up with the Witches' Council and Gunther in the Magical Midway that I didn't even know their relationship had progressed so far?

"Yes," she answered.

"You read my mind?"

"I read your expression, Charlotte, and I've known you long enough to know what you're thinking without needing any magic to tell me," Fiona said, returning from the kitchen with pink cans of some paranormal concoction. "It's rose water delight. It's good for overly emotional women."

"Thanks, I think," I told her, grabbing the can.

"I'm not judging. You have a right to be," she told me. "I feel like I should apologize to you for not being there for you. I thought you had all of this stuff under control, and I realized too late just how much pressure you were under. I clearly was wrong."

"No, you were right. Or at least I thought you were right. This week has been…it's been more than I can take, really. It's just been piling up. I feel like I can't relax for a minute."

"Relax now," Fiona said. She held up the can, and we clinked. "To relaxation."

"Even if it's only for a fleeting moment," I said, taking a sip. It tasted like roses and sugar and something I couldn't place. Fiona was right, though. I felt better. Clearer. Not so weighted down.

"I'm almost afraid to ask you what on earth all of that was. And who was that scary old woman?"

"Ethel Elkins. She's a norn from the Makepeace Circus," I told her. "She's caught up somehow in this Thirteenth Witch prophecy that everyone is all freaking out about."

"And you're the Thirteenth Witch?"

"Honestly? I have absolutely no idea. Maybe? Maybe not? I'm a thirteenth witch, and so is Gunther. Am I *The Thirteenth Witch*? I have no idea. Everyone seems to have a piece of the story, but before this trip, that's all it was. It was just some story I heard vague snippets about here and there. Mostly from Ethel Elkins and her crazy ranting the few times I'd seen her."

"And now?"

"Now, it's…" I couldn't think of the words to explain it, but Fiona just waited. "Now, it's people I don't know closing in around me. Like a noose. I wish that I could slow things down. Go back."

"What would that solve?"

"Nothing. But I was happier before I knew all this."

I *was* happier before I knew this. Even when my father and Uncle Phil fought over my connection to the Magical Midway, even when I first showed up as ringmaster and screwed up one thing after another. None of it felt severe. None of it felt life or death.

Now it all felt serious. It all felt life or death.

And it all felt like it had already been decided for me.

"I'm a control freak," I told Fiona, and she laughed.

"I never would have guessed," she chided.

"No, I mean, I'm used to being in control. Growing up with my witch talents, I just *knew* everything, you know? I knew how the teachers felt, I knew whether kids liked me. I walked through the world with this extra knowledge of what everyone's motivations were. And when I got overwhelmed, my mom was there with her talent to soften my emotions so I could think through almost any situation."

"The world was clear to you and came in measurable waves. Clear, and understandable. Handleable. You're fortunate that you grew up that way, Charlotte."

"Yeah, I mean, I may not like the way certain things unfolded, but I could understand why they did. I had a leg up on everyone else in judging a situation, almost all the time. I had extra help in dealing with things. I always knew the most in nearly every situation, except when I was around my parents."

"And now?"

"Now, I know the least. And it feels like I can't

influence anything anymore. I have all this power, and the least control that I have *ever* had in my entire life, Fiona. Everyone is telling me what I have to do, what I have to save, who I have to be. Heck, even who I'm supposed to marry. And yet I don't understand any of it."

"Uneasy lies the head that wears a crown," Fiona murmured.

"Maybe. I don't know that it's that simple."

"Here's what I know. Are you ready? Do you want to hear it?"

I was touched that Fiona respected my fragile state so much she asked me for permission before unloading all over me with both barrels. It was a very un-Fiona thing to do.

I nodded.

"We are *all* creatures of myth here. We throw ourselves into destinies, into patterns, whether we should or not. We do these things without thinking, ya kin'? It's who we are, who we have always been."

I nodded.

"You're not that. You were born *into* that soil, like us, but you grew under very different sunlight. You lived, you learned, you grew into something…something else. Something just a little bit different. Like us, but not completely like us. Agree?"

"Yeah, I think I get what you're saying."

"Maybe *that* is what you bring to this. Maybe what you are, who you are is *exactly* what you need to be. Maybe that's what the prophecy is about. Maybe you should stop struggling to bury your head back into the soil you came from, Charlotte. Stop trying to give up the control you've learned to have, stop trying to fit *into* the myth."

I stared at Fiona.

"Maybe, ringmaster, you are not supposed to become just like us, a leaf on the wind of destiny ordered about by the universe and beholden to old stories. Maybe you are supposed to stand upon who you are and bring *us* into *your* light."

"You lost me," I told her, tilting my head.

"Don't be who everyone *says* you are supposed to be, Charlotte. Be *who you are*. Maybe that is what will save us."

CHAPTER 14

Fiona and I returned to my yurt after about an hour. The same crowd was there, sitting. Waiting.

Ethel Elkins moved to begin what I assumed was a continuation of whatever statement she felt compelled to make, but a fierce glare from Fiona silenced her.

"Has Faleena showed up yet?" Fiona asked.

"No," Gunther responded.

"Then I suggest we all gab about what the plan is for when she does," Fiona said. "That's the focus right now, and that's the solution we need to come to. We're not going to talk about anything else. No one's going to bring up any other issues with Charlotte until Faleena walks through that yurt door."

"Fiona—"

"I believe Fiona has made it clear what's going to happen," Ningul stated quietly as he rose from his chair. "It is as good a plan as any, and we should follow it."

Fiona smiled gratefully at him across the room.

"Look, we know that she had to be the one that killed Chase. The simplest and most straightforward way to deal with this is to have Gunther freeze her with the lawgiver powers, and compel her to tell us what's going on," I told them.

"Why Gunther and not you?" Fiona asked.

"Whoever catches her takes responsibility for her," I told Fiona. "She has to be maintained within that person's custody, and that person may have to testify or explain to the courts at Democritus what's going on. I don't think that should be me, on the off chance this isn't part of some big magic war with the Witches' Council."

"Fair enough," Fiona said. "Are there any risks we need to know about?"

"If she's a werebear and she's guilty, not really," Gunther said. "The powers are pretty strong against the guilty. If she's guilty, she's subject to them."

"It's that simple?"

"Pretty much, as far as I know," Gunther said. "Mr. Astley, is there anything I'm not clear on that you're aware of?"

"The lawgiver powers are effective against any guilty paranormal. You really just need to let her walk into the room and when she's here, tell her to freeze. She'll freeze, and we've got her," Uncle Phil told him. "It's not much more complicated than that."

"Then we wait, and that's the plan," I said. The group nodded and settled in to wait for Faleena Hobb to arrive.

I walked across the room and sat down beside Gunther. Reaching for his hand, I leaned in so our shoulders touched. "Stay next to me, okay?"

"That's pretty much my goal, Charlotte," he told me smiling.

"No, I don't mean like that," I rolled my eyes and squeezed his hand. "Once Faleena arrives, and this whole thing starts, stay next to me. This all sounds easy, but things never seem to be easy at the Magical Midway. I just want to make sure that if something goes wrong, you're not too far from me."

"Nothing's going to go wrong, Charlotte. Have faith."

"My faith in the universe is a little shaky at the moment."

~

Barely twenty minutes passed before Faleena burst into my tent, breathing heavily, sweat rolling over her chubby cheeks. Her face was flushed as if she'd been running.

"I've been looking all over for you, Anya," she told the naiad. "What are you doing hanging out with this sad looking group? There are at least three parties going on that I know about, and we're invited to all of them."

"Freeze," Gunther said quietly as he stared at the werebear. Her head snapped around swiftly, and she stared daggers at him. Then she smiled. "Freeze," Gunther said more emphatically.

Faleena swung her head to one side and ran her hand through her hair. "Okay, you got me! What is this, some kind of game you all are playing? Do I have to tag someone?"

"Is she not guilty?" Fiona asked, confused.

This was impossible.

There's no one else it could be. I *heard* her.

I jumped off the couch and took three steps that brought me directly in front of Faleena. Grabbing the woman's wrist, I looked her in the eye. She jerked away, but we were locked together.

Magical Midway super-strength. Yay, superpowers.

Opening my mind wide, I focused every bit of intuition and attention on her and whatever she was trying to hide. Sifting through images and emotions as they flowed into me, moving block after block out of the way as if I was tearing down a brick wall by hand. Finally, something broke through.

And then I understood.

"She's guilty," I said. "She's just *not* a werebear."

Faleena yanked her arm from my grasp and stepped back. "That's *awfully* rude, Charlotte. I don't know what kind of ridiculous game you people are playing, but I'll thank you for keeping your hands to yourself."

"I'm not following any of this," Gunther said.

"She's not Faleena," I told Anya. "This is the witch from Impy that got your sister to sell out her fiancé. The one that bought Bolt's ring. The one that sent her back to the Magical Midway to ensure we were vulnerable to the Council by kidnapping Mark."

"I have no idea what she's talking about. Anya, you know me," Faleena told her friend. "You've known me for years!"

"I have, but I…" Anya trailed off as she stared at the woman. "Charlotte, this can't be right. My friend is not a witch."

"This is not your friend, Anya," I told her, and I grabbed for the woman's hand. Yanking it up, I showed Anya the small ring with a tiny blue chip of a stone in the center hidden palm-side on her hand so no one could see it. "This was why the Impy witch wanted Bolt's ring so badly. Just a tiny chip of his ring gives her the power to look like anyone. She's using an elf power to fool everyone."

"She looks like Faleena, but she's not?" Uncle Phil asked.

"Oh, enough of this," Faleena snapped. "Fine, you figured it out; you're all *bloody brilliant*. Did you truly think the Witches' Council was going to give you any quarter, any rest? Any comfort, any time to regroup?"

"But where is Faleena? And who are you?" Anya asked her.

"Your friend is *dead*," the woman shrugged.

"Some magic demands a price. The spell would not work if your chubby friend still breathed the same air."

For a moment, no one reacted.

Then Anya exploded in a rage.

The naiad's hands clawed into the air as she launched toward the woman. Devana jumped in front of my angry friend and stopped her just before she reached the doppelganger of her now lost friend.

"Do you all feel better about yourselves now that you know?" the woman asked them. "Because, truthfully, everyone here knowing means absolutely nothing. Everything I've set up is going to happen, and both of your stupid little circuses will fall."

"Then you may as well tell us the rest of it," Gunther said, clasping his hands politely in front of him. "Our lawgiver powers hold no sway over fellow witches."

"Fellow witches," the woman scoffed. "As if I have anything in common with the three of you."

Ethel Elkins was remarkably silent during this. While I could feel the tension in the room as I sampled everyone witnessing this confrontation, she sat in her chair and had none of their concern. She merely watched as if she was enjoying a play at the theater. There was no tension in her. No fear.

"Why did you kill Chase Trout?" Devana asked.

"The huntress witch speaks," the fake Faleena rolled her eyes. "The Witches' Council has been giving him directives to bring this merry band of bears further into compliance with the expectations of the government. Chase finally balked at the reformations, and the Witches' Council lost its patience. It was hoped that his idiot brother would be more...compliant."

"In other words, he would not bend the knee?"

"He was a bear. He was expected to be on all fours, and he didn't like that," she replied.

"And the framing of Charlotte?" Fiona asked.

"Are you really that stupid, horse, that you need me to explain it?"

"Are you a member of the Witches' Council?" I asked her, cutting off Fiona's next explosion.

"Me? Do you think the Witches' Council members would come to this filthy little corner of the paranormal world and get their hands dirty after their last embarrassment? Oh, that's right, I forgot," she sneered. "You and your little boy toy there are the newest members, so some of them clearly roll in the dirt."

Charlotte, watch her hand.

My gaze dropped down, and I saw her fingers tapping against one another as if she was counting some random pattern. I stepped forward and grabbed her hands in both of mine tightly.

"What's the meaning of this? Let go of me," she snapped, tugging away from me.

"You know, I didn't grow up in the paranormal world, so my first instinct isn't to cast a magic spell. My first instinct is to knock someone's teeth out or break their fingers. I can almost *guarantee* you that I can crush your fingers in my hands faster than you can tap out a spell to get yourself out of this," I told her, squeezing. "So stop tapping and keep talking. What's your name?"

"Alvah," she said tightly.

"Okay, Alvah, you killed Chase Trout under the direction of the Witches' Council, yes?"

"So?"

"So that's against their own law."

"The Witches' Council *makes* the law. The Witches' Council doesn't have to *follow* the law. Why do you think lawgiver powers don't work against witches? And who would believe that they would do such a thing, anyway?"

"Why involve Bolt? Why not just keep the ring and do this without him?"

"The framing of you, for one. We needed to ensure that Wayland and Scout didn't kill one another in a rage while Bolt ensured that no one could possibly be suspected for the murder other than you. Only elves and your mother can *manipulate* people's emotions and feelings in such a way, so he was necessary."

"Charlotte, please ask her to change back," Anya said through angry tears. "I don't know that I can contain myself if she continues to wear the face of my friend."

I twisted the woman's hands and grabbed the ring in my fingers. With a tug and a flash, Faleena Hobb disappeared. An ugly looking short woman stood in the center of my yurt where the werebear had been.

"That's mine!" she shouted, her voice shaking with rage. Alvah clawed at my hands, and her fingers raked against me. The sound of nails against metal made a horrible screeching noise.

And then I got an idea.

I popped the ring in my mouth. Opening it, I showed her the ring sitting in the center of my tongue. She reached quickly to grab it and howled as her outstretched fingers slammed against the invisible metal barrier that encased me.

"You broke my hand!" she screamed.

I know, I know. It was juvenile.

But I enjoyed it.

I turned away from her and quickly spit the ring into my palm, pocketing it before she could see what I did with it. "I believe you did that to yourself," I told her.

"You will pay for what you did! They will arrest you! Bolt and I are protected by the Witches' Council! No one will believe you even if you told them what happened. Not even witches are thought to have the power that I have!"

"Right," Gunther said. "And you are right, Alvah, I can't use my lawgiver powers on you. Even if I could, it's not like I have anywhere to take you. I do, though, have this."

Gunther held his palm up and whispered a word. Light streamed like a projector from his lawgiver ring replaying the entire scene we had witnessed from the moment he crossed his hands in front of him. The words spoken just moments ago bounced off the light.

My jaw dropped.

"Didn't know it could do that, did you?" Gunther asked me and winked.

"You think you've won," Alvah growled. "You haven't won *anything*. The Witches' Council is determined to stop you and anyone else that questions their rightful leadership. They may have failed this time, but they, too, have their prophecies and I promise you will fail."

"What do *you* know about prophecies?"

"Oh no," Alvah said, walking backward toward the door. "Now that I know you are recording this, I will say no more. I'm sure the norn will be happy to guide you directly into your doom."

"Are we just letting her leave?" Anya asked as she squirmed in Devana's grasp.

"She's right," I told my friend. "We can't hold her with the lawgiver power, and handing her over to the Witches' Council for prosecution would be a joke even if we could. Let her go. Let her run back to Impy and tell the Council how she failed."

"We'll bring the recording to Scout," Gunther said as Alvah turned and fled from the yurt. "That should help the werebears and Wayland understand what happened to Chase, and clear Charlotte of any wrongdoing."

"Maybe it will help the werebears understand that the Witches' Council is corrupt," I added.

"If this doesn't do it, I honestly don't know what would," Uncle Phil said.

It took some insistence on Devana's part to get Scout Trout to sit with us and watch the images contained within Gunther's ring. Once he did, though, I was a psychic witness to the most dramatic transformation of a sentient being I had ever sensed.

Scout Trout went into the meeting with us a playboy, a spoiled and angry hothead.

He emerged as a leader.

"I don't understand," Scout said, looking to Devana. "You are working with them?"

"I came here because of a prophecy, Scout," she told him gently. "While I have enjoyed our time together, I must admit that I had more than one agenda with regards to our relationship. I needed to ensure that you did not prevent what must come to pass for all of our people. Now that has been fulfilled, and I'm afraid our time must come to an end. I am needed elsewhere."

The handsome werebear swallowed and nodded. Any hurt he felt over Devana's confession was well hidden, and he handled it maturely and with no resentment. "Thank you for letting me know," he told her quietly. "I wish you the luck of the bear on your journey."

"Thank you, friend," she nodded.

"I can't say that I am surprised by what you have told me," Scout said turning back to me. "I began to sense that the conspiracy surrounding my brother's death was deeper than I first thought."

Wayland snorted, and Scout's eyes raised to look the huge paranormal directly in his eye. "You have something to say, cyclops?"

"You know, he was killed because they thought you would be more pliable," Wayland snapped at him. "If you weren't such an idiot, maybe he would still be alive."

"If I wasn't such an idiot, we would probably *both* be dead," Scout countered. "It doesn't sound to me like the Witches' Council is flippantly murdering in one-offs. These women mean business."

Wayland blinked his one big eye and shrugged.

"Where is Bolt? We may not be able to bring Alvah to justice, but surely we can arrest that elf," Scout said.

"Arrest him for what?"

"He knew about the murder. He was a part of it, wasn't he? For what he did to Ms. Astley? Surely there must be something."

"Even if we did, where would we bring him?" Gunther asked Scout. "You hand all of your criminals over to the legal system in Impy, which is controlled entirely by the Witches' Council. I doubt he'd make it five minutes after we dropped him off at the jail. They would release him, or they'd kill him because he knew too much."

"Are you telling me that no one will pay for my brother's murder?"

The question landed with a thud in the center of the group. Wayland and Scout both looked to Gunther, Devana and me for some way to balance the scales, some way to see justice done, but Gunther was right. I saw no way it was possible. At least not possible for now.

"This afternoon, you will become leader," Wayland said, his voice gruff and thick with anger and regret. "You will stop being an idiot. You will *grow up*. You will *not* get yourself killed. And you'll remember this. I have a feeling that you will be faced with a moment when you can get justice and honor your brother. Recognize it when it comes. And take it."

"It's not right," Scout said.

"Nothing about this situation is right," I told him gently.

"Why are you helping us?" Scout asked suddenly. "You're witches. All three of you. Why are you going against your own?"

"The Witches' Council are *not* my own," I said.

"There is a corruption in the balance," Devana said. "The prophecy says that it has a chance to be set right. We are a part of that."

"The Witches' Council says we get what they give us," Scout responded.

"The Witches' Council is wrong," Gunther told him.

"That's treason. You're speaking treason," Scout warned him quietly.

"Treason is killing. Violating the law of the land that you created, that you make everyone else follow. To me, *that* is treason. No leader should be above the law," Gunther said with a faraway look. After a second, he refocused and looked Scout in the eye. "But yes, technically you're right. What I just said is treason."

"Then we stand with you in your rebellion," Scout said.

"That, too, is a dangerous statement, friend," Devana told him. "Are you sure? Are you sure that you wish to stand with us? Even saying this privately…truth has a way of traveling."

"My brother died defending our clan from those witches," Scout told her. "I will not dishonor him by doing less for my people."

Wayland wiped a colossal tear from his sizable single eye.

"He would be proud," Wayland told Scout.

CHAPTER 15

THE CLEARING ON TOP OF BIG BEAR MESA SEEMED
filled with clusters of werebears as far as the eye
could see. Gunther, Devana and I hung toward
the back. We were honored that we had been
invited to witness this event, but we didn't want
to intrude.

A ten by ten cut tree trunk served as the small
stage. Scout made his way toward it quietly, and
those witnessing quieted as he drew closer. Some
people wiped tears away, others frowned. Some
people looked angry.

"Is he crowned?" I whispered to Gunther.

"No," he whispered back. "Watch."

Scout stepped up onto the trunk stage with
some assistance from his guards, stepping to the

front and facing the crowd. He smiled at them and then bowed.

To my surprise, he dropped to one knee before all those gathered, and only then did he speak.

"I honor all the bears of our clan," Scout said clearly. "Whether black bears or brown bears, panda bears or polar bears, sloth or spectacled or sun bears, we are all of the same clan. We are bear!"

"We are bear!" the crowd called back, raising their fists in the air. He bowed his head at their call and then continued.

"Whether we walk on four legs or two, whether we live in skin or fur, whether we roam the forests or the streets, we are bear!"

"We are bear!" the crowd roared as he bowed.

"We honor where we came from, we honor what we are, we honor and protect our brothers and sisters that can shift no more. We are bear!"

"We are bear!" the crowd shouted. A mix of close and distant roars echoed up and over the mesa to wash over all those gathered in the clearing. As the bellows surrounding us quieted, those assembled shimmered into their bear forms and roared back in response. It sent chills down my spine.

"Are those people that couldn't fit up here?" I asked Gunther.

"No, Charlotte," Gunther smiled, his eyes twinkling. "Those are non-paranormal bears. The bears in this forest have gathered to witness and acknowledge the new leader."

I glanced toward the edges of the forest and realized that dark faces with shining eyes stared out from the trees. There were hundreds of them hiding within the leaves.

A tall man stepped forward to stand next to Scout. "Our bear brothers have accepted the new leader," he shouted to the silent crowd. "Our bear sisters have called out their approval. It is now up to the shifter clan to accept the oath of the one who wants to lead. He may rise and make his case."

The man placed his hand on Scout's shoulder, and the werebear rose. He scanned the faces in the crowd, nodding as he recognized friends or family members. Then, with a deep breath, he began.

"I am not worthy," he said. "My brother was a better leader than me. I know that. I know that I am not the first choice of many here. I also can't blame you at all for having your doubts about me. I have been selfish, a royal brat that enjoyed my privilege as my brother did the work to maintain us as the strong clan we are. He worked hard for you. He died drawing a line in the sand." Scout's voice trailed off.

"I can't be my brother. But I can honor my brother's sacrifice by oathing to you that I will spend the rest of my days fighting for our clan. Protecting our cubs, and defending our way of life," he shouted angrily.

"We are bears! We are not witches, we are not paranormals, we are bears! We have been as long as the forests have been, and we will be as long as they stand. Like the trees that shelter us, we are an evergreen people. We change to evolve, not to lose who and what we are!"

Those listening to Scout nodded in agreement.

"I ask you to allow me to ascend to Cavemaster, to guard our hearth, to keep safe our home, and to judge when we must emerge and defend it from those that would collapse it around us. May I serve you? Will you allow me to take up my brother's right?" Scout shouted, jumping to the front of the tree trunk and holding his arms out to his people.

A howl went up as drums beat and rattles

shook. The werebears accepted Scout, and he bowed to them on his knees in thanks.

"I thank you," Scout said. The tall man extended his hand and placed a ring upon Scout's finger. He raised his hand high in the air, and golden beams of light shot out in every direction, bathing the celebrants in a warm glow. Trees shook as the bears banged against them.

"That," I said, exhaling, "was amazing."

"It's not over yet," Gunther said and pointed to Scout.

Scout jumped off the stage and was walking directly toward us as people shook his hand and pounded his shoulder in congratulations. He took nearly five minutes to cross the clearing, picking his way through the crowd, but he finally made it and faced us.

"Thank you for waiting," Scout said to the three of us.

"No problem. I caught the signal," Gunther said. "Congratulations, by the way. That was an incredible ceremony."

"Thank you," Scout nodded. "As my first act as Cavemaster, I wish to extend honorary membership in the bear clan, to you and Gunther and Devana. I don't know if I would have ever known the truth of my brother's murder if it wasn't for you."

"We would be honored, Cavemaster." Devana bowed her head. Gunther and I bowed as well.

Without a speech or ceremony, Scout placed his hand upon each of our foreheads, starting with me. A spark of golden light flashed for just a moment as he touched me, and a golden warmth spread across my skin.

"You will always have safety in our caves," he said. Scratching his head, he leaned forward looking regretful. "Normally, that ceremony is a bit longer and a bit more formal, but now that we have a Cavemaster, my brother and Faleena must be honored without any more delay."

"I understand," I told him.

"Even so, I wanted to start my service off with something more positive. I couldn't think of anything my brother would appreciate more than honoring those who honored him." Scout brushed away an escaped tear. "You'll join us for the memorial?"

"Wouldn't miss it," I said.

Scout left and walked toward the tall man, and the three of us walked back toward the Magical Midway.

"It feels unfinished," I told Gunther and Devana as we walked.

"People have died, and no one of the living has paid the price other than those that loved them," Devana said. "It is unbalanced. The justice that should have been? It tugs at you, ringmaster. You can sense the imbalance."

"Please, call me Charlotte," I told the fierce woman.

"Perhaps I will," Devana said and smiled.

Chase Trout couldn't be laid to rest until his brother had taken his place as Cavemaster. Although Chase had been the leader of the bear clan, he and Faleena shared a memorial service in honor of their sacrifice for their people.

Many people, both bear shifters and Magical Midway citizens, attended to honor them both.

Anya was as upset as I'd ever seen her. The naiad was wracked with guilt that she hadn't recognized a stranger looking out from her friend's eyes. Coming so fast on the heels of her sister Alexa's betrayal of the Magical Midway, it was yet another blow to the tough woman.

Her gentle friend, Avalon, stood beside her while she wept.

"I think Anya may have the most trouble getting over this," Gunther told me. "All of the major events that have happened since you arrived touched her deeply."

"Is that so?" Devana asked, turning to gaze at Anya's retreat. "How well do you know her?"

"Well enough," I told Devana.

"Perhaps," she answered.

"You seem to say that a lot," I said as the three of us walked slowly back to the Magical Midway. "I feel like every time you say that there are a hundred things in your head that you're choosing not to tell us."

"Perhaps," she smiled.

"I really think that's gonna start to bug me awful fast."

"So what do we do now?" Gunther asked.

"Well, are you really going to stay at the Magical Midway? I know that Ethel Elkins decided that we're all gonna be roomies, but I feel like your dad is not going to be thrilled at the idea."

"Probably not," Gunther said. "I can see some advantages to it, though. We have to go to Imperatorial City in a month or so for the

Council meeting, and we're not prepared. Well, we *were* prepared. I think this week has changed a lot of things. Our approach may have been..."

"Too respectful?"

"I guess that's one way to put it," Gunther smiled.

"I will be attending you in Imperatorial City," Devana said as we walked. "Part of my role here is to ensure the protection of the both of you, as well as to witness what is to come."

I stopped walking and stepped back to look at Devana. She slowed and then turned back around to face me. With her hands folded in front of her and her head held high, she looked like a queen.

"Are you on our side?" I asked her.

"Of course," she answered.

"No perhaps? You're just flat out on our side?"

"I serve the balance, ringmaster. You are working toward the balance, and so I am on your side," she said.

"If I wake up tomorrow and decide to, I don't know, put my thumb on a hypothetical scale?"

"If you wake up tomorrow and you no longer serve the balance, if your motives are no longer correct, if your goal is no longer moral and righteous, then no, ringmaster. I would no longer be on your side."

"That's a pretty fickle ally," Gunther said after considering her words.

"When has *any* war had anything other than fickle allies, Mr. Makepeace?" Devana asked him. "We all serve who and what we serve, do we not?"

"Perhaps," I answered. She raised her eyebrow as we stepped across the barrier and reentered the Magical Midway.

We are in your yurt already, Samson said as soon as my foot hit the path. *Fiona, Ningul, your uncle, and I. Anya has retired to her yurt with Avalon. Alessandra is taking care of her.*

Thanks for the update, but do we have a meeting or something?

Your uncle wants to talk to you about the new additions to the Magical Midway. As you can imagine—

I can speak for myself, Samson. Charlotte, get here as soon as you can. Without Gunther, Devana, or that obnoxious old woman, please.

I'm on my way.

Though I must admit, I wasn't all that excited about going.

"Everything okay?" Gunther asked.

"It appears that the peanut gallery is waiting for me in my yurt, and they have requested that I attend this little shindig without either of you."

"That's not surprising, ringmaster," Devana said. "In fact, I'm glad they are concerned. It shows they have a sense of awareness of the seriousness of the situation."

"I'm glad you approve," I told her. "I'm going to head over there."

"Between the three of you, I can't get a word in edgewise!" I hollered over the small crowd that certainly didn't sound small.

"There are four of us, Charlotte," Fiona said.

"Yes, but Ningul isn't biting my head off, so I didn't count him. You and Uncle Phil are talking over each other and Samson figured he just sneak into my head."

Guardianship has its privileges, Samson said.

"Look, I don't know much about this prophecy, and for the most part, you all know what I know at this point. Actually, you probably know more, because if history is any indication, somebody in this room is withholding something from me that I probably really need to know," I said, pointedly staring at my uncle.

"Charlotte, we just don't know much about these people."

"We know Gunther, and frankly if his dad's cool with him staying at the Magical Midway that probably works out much better for us, anyway. He and I have a whole lot of work to do before we go to the Witches' Council meeting and not a lot of time to do it in," I pointed out.

"And you don't think having your boyfriend here is going to be a distraction?" Uncle Phil asked me.

"I don't think whether my boyfriend is staying on *my* Magical Midway or not is, frankly, *any* of your business. We are so past the 'woops, Charlotte dropped the carousel in Egypt' level of complications and problems. The training wheels are off."

"Well, it's not like we have to worry about the two of you…well…you know…" Uncle Phil sat down and crossed his arms.

"No, I don't know."

"You two can't…Oh, come on, Charlotte, are you going to make me say it?"

"What your uncle is trying to *avoid* saying is that you and Gunther have no *ability* to consummate your relationship. You no doubt would have figured this out, if you *really* thought about the situation with the kiss, but you've been distracted," Fiona said.

"The kiss? I don't understand what…"

I didn't understand. And then, suddenly, I did.

Oh my God.

"Yes, you do. You're lucky he was polite and just went in with his lips. If he'd gone in with a lot of tongue, well…" Fiona held out her hands. "That boy might not have been able to speak for a week. And you should be very, *very* grateful that he didn't point something else at you."

Oh my God.

"The damage that could have been done—"

"Oh my God, you have to stop talking," I whispered. My face felt like an exploding tomato again.

"Just as long as we're clear. I don't want anything getting *damaged*," Fiona said. "You *do* understand what I'm trying to tell you, Charlotte, right? I just want to be sure that you understand your little metal robot psychic shield thing extends all the way to—"

"*Oh, please, please, for the love of all that is holy and all that is good in this world, please, Fiona, stop talking!*"

"It's a safety issue, is all I'm saying," she said, settling back on the couch. Ningul wrapped his arm around her and hushed her.

"Oh, *now* you're jumping in to tell her to be quiet?"

"I'm sorry, Charlotte, but I do have to agree with Fiona," Ningul said as he shifted uncomfortably next to her. "Just thinking about it makes me—"

"Stop thinking about it. Stop thinking about it, stop talking about it. In fact, never talk about it again."

"Do you think I should have a talk with Gunther?" Ningul asked.

"I will banish you both from this midway," I warned him.

"I think Charlotte can handle it, dear," Fiona told him, patting his hands. "It was lovely of you to offer."

"Of course, anything for Charlotte," Ningul said and nodded.

If I close my eyes and click my heels three times, maybe I can get back to Kansas.

You never lived in Kansas, Samson said, confused.

Forget it.

"I've heard your concerns. But right now, Gunther being here is practical, Devana being here will allow us to understand her motivations more, and Ethel Elkins being here…"

"Will drive us all crazy, you realize that, don't you, Charlotte?" Uncle Phil said.

"Maybe," I told him. "But she saw me that first night I went to the Makepeace Circus. She saw me when she wasn't supposed to see me. That woman knows things. She's come to me in dreams, and she's known Gunther since he was a child and has never harmed him in any way."

"You think Roland will go for it?" Fiona asked.

"I don't know," I shrugged. "I'll let Gunther deal with explaining all of this to his father. Devana and Ethel claim they are bound to the Magical Midway, anyway. If they are, and I can't affect that bond, they're going to move with us no matter what."

"So don't bond them," Uncle Phil said. "Let's see if they move with us."

"Okay."

"Where are we going to next?" Uncle Phil asked. "We don't have any fairs scheduled for several months, though we could pop up somewhere."

"I'm going to get a hold of Mom and Dad. I think we're going to head back to Mickwac. I haven't spent any time with my parents for a while, and I want to check their wards. Since the Magical Midway financially supports the animal shelter, maybe I can give it added protection somehow. I can't believe if this gets much worse that they won't be a target again."

"Never thought of that. The wards issue, I mean. That's possible," Uncle Phil said, thinking.

"You never *had* to think of it. No one wanted to squash us like bugs until I showed up."

CHAPTER 16

"It looks fine," Fiona said as she took in the larger room.

As everyone at the Magical Midway was milling about saying goodbye to the new werebear friends they had made, I was remodeling my yurt. The rustic one-room traveling tent was transformed into a four bedroom home with a large common area in the center.

It still looked like a yurt from the outside. In fact, it looked like one-quarter of a yurt only from the outside. Inside, I had added thousands of square feet and living quarters for Devana, Ms. Elkins, and Gunther.

"It looks like a college dormitory from that

movie that you showed me on your carry glass," Fiona observed. "It even has a library in the corner and everything."

I told her it was a tablet. She told me she had never seen a stone that looked like that. I gave up. Carry glass it is.

"Gunther and I were really stretched for space before this ever started," I told her. "So, this actually isn't half bad. It's not like I ever had any privacy in my yurt, anyway."

"And the kitchen is fantastic," she said. "The table is much more suitable considering how much we use it."

Devana came out of her room and bowed to me in thanks. "My sleeping quarters are wonderful, Charlotte. I am incredibly grateful that you have gone to such trouble."

"No problem," I told her.

"With all the bedrooms right off of the main room, we should all be able to meet whenever we need to without much complication," Fiona said.

"Are you in here often?" Devana asked, tilting her head.

"I'm in here enough," Fiona answered with a smile that was as fake as a three dollar bill. "I'm sure we will spend *lots* of time getting to know each other!"

"Perhaps," Devana answered. She bowed and walked back to her room.

"I don't trust that woman," Fiona said quietly.

"Anything in particular?"

"It takes a troublemaker to know a troublemaker. She's a troublemaker."

"Well, so am I, if you really think about it."

"Oh, Charlotte, you stumble back into trouble. That woman flings it out in front of her and then jumps in after it."

Gunther walked into my yurt and paused so quickly that he skidded on the new wooden floor. "Am I in the right place?"

"If by the right place you mean the ringmaster's new gorgeous four bedroom house, absolutely. You're totally in the right place," I told him. "What do you think?"

"I think you did a great job, Charlotte. Wow, these floors look just like the floors from our cabin back at the Makepeace Circus," Gunther said. "Nice job."

"Is your dad okay with you staying here for a while?"

"Yeah, he wasn't thrilled at the reason for it. He's concerned about the Witches' Council's escalation of attacks, obviously. But he said he could do without me for a month or so. He just wants me to keep in touch and keep them informed of what's going on."

"That's your room," I told him and pointed to a door on the far right.

"My room?" he asked.

"Yep. That's yours, there's mine, Devana is over there, and Ethel's in there. I think she liked it. She grunted and then went in slamming the door, and she hasn't come out yet. So, I'll take that as she probably likes it."

"Oh," he said. "I see."

Well, don't act so excited. Sheesh.

"Each bedroom is pretty big and has a sitting area with a pullout couch in case we need to bunk people in with us," I told him. "Did you bring Delilah with you?"

Oh no. I don't know why I didn't think about that. But I didn't think about that, Samson said as he jumped down off the new sectional couch and trotted toward my closed bedroom door. *Cat door? Did you really make a door that closes without a cat door?*

With all your superpowers, Samson, you can't open a door?

Make a cat door, please.

I waved my hand, and a cat-sized flap appeared in my heavy wooden bedroom door. I motioned toward Gunther's door and installed one there as well.

Thank you. Going to try out the new king size bed. You kept my favorite pillow, didn't you?

Yes, Samson.

Samson's lithe black body disappeared through the door.

Gunther had pulled out his kitten, and Delilah was squeaking after Samson as he disappeared.

"Tomorrow, Delilah," I told the kitten.

"You understood her?"

"Remember, I grew up in an animal shelter. I speak cat even when they can't shout into my mind."

"Right, then," Gunther said as he looked at his closed bedroom door. "I guess I should head off to bed. Good night, Fiona. Charlotte."

As the door closed, Fiona turned to me. "That man was not expecting and did not want his own bedroom," she told me. "Did you not talk to him about the sleeping arrangements before you did all this?"

"No," I whispered to her, grabbing her arm and heading to the opposite end of the room away from Gunther's bedroom. "Us moving in together was not exactly an option that I wanted to entertain, Fiona."

"You haven't told him about the shield, have you," she whispered back. I shook my head no. "Oh, Charlotte, I know I teased you about it, but you have to tell the man."

"How do you have a conversation with someone you may be falling in love with to tell them that if they try to be intimate with you, it will break their…I mean, how does someone even broach that?"

"You just do," Fiona said, embracing me. "Oh, my friend. I am so sorry for the complications that you have to endure."

"Thanks," I squeaked.

"You two will work it out," she said as we pulled apart. "There's an answer to all this, Charlotte, I know there is. And if anyone can find that answer, it's you."

Go grab *Go for the Juggler*, the next book in the Magical Midway series right now!

KEEP UP WITH LEANNE LEEDS

Thanks so much for reading! I hope you liked it! Want to keep up with me? Text me at 1-512-359-3123 to get updates, info, or to shoot me a question!

You can also visit leanneleeds.com to:

Find all my books…

Sign up for my newsletter…

Like me on Facebook…

Follow me on Twitter…

Follow me on Instagram…

Thanks again for reading!

Leanne Leeds

FIND A TYPO? LET US KNOW!

Typos happen. It's sad, but true.

Though we go over the manuscript multiple times, have editors, have beta readers, and advance readers, it's inevitable that determined typos and mistakes sometimes find their way into a published book.

Did you find one? If you did, think about reporting it on leanneleeds.com so we can get it corrected.

www.ingramcontent.com/pod-product-compliance
Lightning Source LLC
Chambersburg PA
CBHW031606240626
47153CB00002B/644